To Trish,
Enjoy
the reading
- FAB

THIS BOOK

JUST MIGHT

BE BATS* CRAZY**

© Fatima Al Badran

©2023

Independently published

Preface

Hello. What you are about to read is a compilation of short stories that my professors had to endure reading during my years at Brunel University. These tales branch out to multiple genres and subgenres so you never really know what to expect to read until you begin. Some may have been inspired upon movies while others take on their own life I like to think, originating from the wonderfully frightening ideas that come with the influence of leg medication for my Cerebral Palsy. Think of this collection as your own Russian nesting doll. Just be warned that once you begin, you might not be able to put the book down. It is simply yourself and mind boggling tales from here on out. I have added caution warnings for stories that might be too explicitly gory or contain light sexual content. With that all said, step forth into this literal four sided universe of madness, mayhem and unexplanatory, strange, weirdness.

Personally I love every single tale within this book. To pick just one would be like asking a mother to pick between her children. One tale however, that gets a chuckle out of me each time I revisit it has to be 'A Night Out with the Broskies' just from how absurd and funny the premise is. My mind always goes to 'sexy transformer' whenever that cabinet transforms, only instead of action music, it's sultry burlesque music.

These tales are no stranger to getting freaky, and fast. (Even the content page is all askew, (just like the short stories featured in this collection.)

- Fatima Al Badran (the author with the unhinged imagination)

CONTENTS

3

4

More by this Author   Pg200

DNE

The slithering, moulded, fanged abomination lets out an ear-piercing shrill as it finally succumbs to its death among the flames, thanks to Tyler. Its flesh-like exterior begins to crisp into fragments of dust. The screams of the creature soon fade into oblivion. - Tyler might or might not be a pyromaniac now. We're alive. That's what matters. Bruised, sure. Exhausted like hell, but alive all the same. Ten hours ago, we were average students. Now, we're survivors.

I'm leaning by the wall of the broken homeroom class. While the ceiling took damage from the hell-spawn's rampage, leaving us with an open roof, the walls of the room somehow managed to uphold themselves through the war. They're a bit bloody though, so Tyler's taking care of that for me. Anything to keep him away from fire.

All that remains of this school are two cubicles. Me, Tyler and Chloe have taken shelter in the homeroom while Elly and Steven have taken shelter in the room next door to us, also known as the remains of what used to be the Spanish classroom.

7

Unlike us, their room somehow has a ceiling. We can hear their flirting. Meanwhile, I'm about to collapse.

"Why the hell did they get the room with the ceiling?!"

"Can it, Tyler. They wanted privacy."

"Privacy?! Look, I'm the one who saved her life from that…that thing, and instead of a thanks, Elly's busy sucking Steven's face off!"

"Someone sounds jealous ~"

"And that's my cue to leave."

Shuffling onto my feet in order to get away from Tyler's complaining, I find refuge in the corner of the room near the only working radiator in the whole building. At least he's not playing with fire anymore. Leaning my back onto the warmth, my nerves begin to fade. As my eyelids grow heavy, I take a moment to breathe deeply - something I haven't done all day.

Every limb in my body aches. It's from all that damn running I had to do while luring that demon into 'whatever's left of the school's atrium'.

My shoulder begins tensing up. I wince under my breath.

"Atch-"

I remove my sleeve and notice the red bite mark from before, slowly beginning to throb. That's what I get for saving my girlfriend's life. A fucked-up shoulder. Probably infected by now.

Always the hero, huh. Gotta bear the pain. You're the leader. Everyone's counting on you.

Covering my shoulder, I lean back, about to fall into a hazy dream, only to hear America's sweetheart's moans getting louder and louder. While I don't give two shits about what they're doing, Tyler on the other hand- poor guy. He wastes no time in, and I kid you not, screaming from the top of his lungs:

"Can you two chill out with your moaning?!"

To this, he receives the finger from Stephen through the glass slit in the door, now blurred by their sweat. They're really going to town – and I don't blame them. Sure, it sounds like two dogs fighting over a bone, but honestly, I'd be the same if I thought Chloe was consumed by a demonic hell-spawn. Young damn love.

9

Chloe chimes in to reduce the flames.

"Tyler, let them be."

"I've 'let them be' since middle school…I-I'm gonna lose it."

There's desperation in his voice. He's close to tears. I can hear it. Whoever said men don't cry can go fuck themselves.

He turns to me, dejected.

"G…Gray?"

Crap. I can't afford for him to lose it right now. He's too much of a hot head.

"Chlo, come help me cover up the glass."

She nods, as we both push whatever's left of the bookshelf in front of the door. As we push the last inch of the wooden shelf, the walls stop moving.

I guess hornydum and hornydee must be done doing the tango. Their moans continue wailing through the walls.

Are you fu-

I turn 'round to see Tyler flickering a lighter in his hand.

"Make 'em stop, Gray!"

Tyler's about to lose it. I make my way to the door to tell 'Romeo and Juliet' to pack it in. Just as I'm about to do so, Steven's moans suddenly become quieter. We all pause and look up. After a few seconds, we hear muffled screams.

"Mphhh!"

What kinda kinky stuff are they into?!

I waste no time in attempting to move the bookshelf. Meanwhile Chloe uses a desk near the wall to try and climb over to peek at what's happening. I'm near Tyler, trying to retrieve his lighter. He's shaking at this point. The groans from next door grow even louder than before. A familiar ear-piercing shrill bursts through the walls.

"Something's got my leg! Gray!"

I notice Chloe being pulled over the wall into the other room.

"M-My leg!"

She cries out for me as a CRACK sound can be heard.

"Chlo!"

While panicking, I try to grab her hand but miss by an inch.

With Chloe's body now hauled in the other room, Elly begins snarling. I hear Steven choking and gasping for air. It sounds like someone's stabbing him. Chloe lets out a loud, pain-filled scream.

My ears start ringing.

"Tyler, put that Goddamn lighter down and help me move the bookshelf!"

Rushing to the door, Tyler and I manage to move the bookshelf together and break the glass to rescue both Steven and Chloe, only to see Elly salivating over a freshly mutilated corpse with blond hair.

Chlo has blond hair…

I stand frozen, my breath quickening with anger and fear. My knees grow weak.

By 'Elly's' mouth, hangs a dismembered leg. It's being gnawed at and has a tattoo of a crimson skull on it. – It matches the one Stephen's got.

Tyler finds himself walking towards the direction of the thing that resembles 'Elly.' I watch in terror as he squats over Chloe's mutilated corpse and licks his lips with hunger.

He then turns to me.

Oscar's Possession

"Stop kidding around, Oscar," but I was met with only silence. I watched my friend on the floor lie in a puddle of dirt. His body bent inwards and still. As his bottom lip quivered with motion, no words left them. His skin was grazed by the pavement that he hit, still his eyes were open. His brown pupils were rolled back, so that the bloody veins under his eyes was all I saw.

I wish things ended here.

"Help him up, come on."

I leaned over the threshold and offered him my hand, but it was already too late. Oscar started convulsing violently, as if he was possessed. Fearing my own life, I flinched back into the crowd, taking in the sight,

Five seconds of shaking, then, nothing.

14

The crowd watched on in horror as Oscar's mouth slowly opened. A high-pitched screech came out, the same sound when you scrape chalk on a chalkboard. We covered our ears from the piercing groan, but it only got louder. I fell to my knees as my head began to pound.

"Ah! Stop him! Someone stop him!"

No one listened to me. My heartbeat increased and only added to the pounding. I braced my head, slapping the sides to stop the madness. The screeching continued even after I blocked it out. It got louder and louder until it was the only thing I could hear.

I couldn't hear my own heartbeat or breath anymore. There was only the painful screeching of chalk followed by Oscar's limp body which began slowly levitating.

I watched through widened eyes as his torso violently slammed back and forth onto the road. I was paralysed with fear at the sight as I watched my friend's spine crack with every slam. It sounded like glass shattering over the road. His mother wailed at the sight of her son.

"Help him! Help my boy, please!"

15

As his body threw itself downwards onto the road in repeat, blood emerged from out of his limbs. With every slam, more blood spewed from his torso, to the point where it flowed out of him like a fountain.

He hauled onto the road with such a violent pressure, that I heard his skull slamming against the hard floor. I stood there covered in blood as the crowd screamed at the sight of the torn apart body that was twisted in front of them. He was as light as a paper bag and as pale as a corpse, completely drained of any signs of life within him.

The demon was not done yet. To make sure Oscar had no chance of being saved, his body stopped hovering. Instead, it was stretched to the point where I swear that I heard his own limbs rip out from his arm and leg sockets.

His flesh kept stretching and stretching until his body was ripped into two in front of my very eyes. The tendons within his flesh tore apart like paper. The crowd fell silent as a puddle of blood formed around Oscar's disregarded flesh travelled to their feet. I felt my breakfast rise up at the sight and held my reflex back. There was only silence.

16

No one believed that in a few minutes, all that was left of little Oscar Kale was a bloody pile of flesh. The crowd was filled with retching spectators, friends of Oscar's, his family and his teachers.

The town priest walked up to the pile of flesh on the ground and threw matches over it. Oscar's remains were lit ablaze in a cloud of heat. I gagged at the sight and covered my mouth with my sleeve as the stench burned at the back of my nostrils.

"Begone, foul demon! This boy will not see the likes of heaven!"

The flames roared through the watching eyes of the priest, who looked onwards at Oscar's remains in disgust.

My Phasing Sanity

My husband places a soft kiss on the side of my cheek while rolling over towards me. He pulls me into a warm embrace, which startles me at first, till I find myself melting in the familiar warmth of his arms.

"Mike, she's crying again."

"Let's just say it's because 'Brian the Bear' had to take a trip to the dryer."

Surprised by this, I turn to Mike with a fake shocked expression.

"You absolute *monster~*"

"She kept drooling on that thing. I had no choice."

"Honey, you know that's her favourite toy. She's practically obsessed with it, no wonder she's crying."

"I'll make it up to her later. Can't we just get a few more minutes in?"

I sit up with unkempt hair and kick my marital sloth off the bed. He lets out a groan as his face meets the floor, only to then get up and scratch his messy hair.

"Fine, I'm going, but *once I return*, I'll get you back for that~"

While he leaves the room to check on our daughter, I take the opportunity to stretch over to his side. I close my eyes, soon drifting back into slumber. In that moment, as the world around me fades into a haze of mist, I hear my father's voice.

"Look at me, Jennifer. For God's sake, look at me so that your mother can come back to me!"

Within the dream, I see a vision of my bedroom which is suddenly covered in fragments of distorted black squares. I then see myself. A sharp pain surges through my forehead, where a mechanical implant lies.

I feel my weight become lighter while my vision falters rapidly, leaving me in darkness. With the last of its remaining strength, the darkness around me fades into transparent rays of light which shape out faint blue outlines.

19

The eye blinks to focus its parameter and length of vision onto the outlines, which soon appear as familiar figures within the mapped-out field of vision. While seeing all this, I'm submerged in a void of whiteness. The outlines act out various moments which I recall from my memories, such as implanting a foreign object into the other outline's forehead. The object itself is burned onto my mechanical retina as a blue smudge.

The void suddenly throws me backwards with such a strong gravitational force that my vision glitches. The eye opens to a new scene, where outlines of blue surround the white void.

There's now a faint bed, faint trolly of surgical equipment and the blue outlined figure operating on the small, outlined figure. My vision zooms itself into the surgical procedure, making note and registering how the small figure's visual nerves respond to being connected to the mechanical implant.

I'm suddenly transported to glitching images of my

dear family which fill the walls of the void. My husband and I are surrounded by a forest. I'm cradling something in my arms. My vision tries to focus the image into fruition, yet the glitches keep the image from being seen.

I see myself in my daughter's room, only my daughter is now left on the floor, screaming. Her cot is torn to bits while I watch my daughter fade away before my very eyes.

The eye blinks. The floor becomes submerged in whiteness. My heart sinks.

"It can't be true! N-no, please!"

I wake up abruptly with tears trickling down my eyes. The sensation of a stronger electrical current courses through my head. I look around the room, noticing streaks of black lines suddenly appear within our cream-coloured walls.

My husband kneels by my side, concerned. I take a deep breath and exhale slowly before coming to my senses that I had a nightmare. I place my hand on his shoulder, yet the speed of my blink is slower than usual.

My eyes open to my husband beginning to fade

21

away.

No...I must still be dreaming!

I reach out for him. His hand which caresses my cheek, passes through my fingertips, like the trick of light. As an electrical surge shocks my forehead without warning, enveloping me into total darkness for a split second, otherworldly voices begin conversing in murmurs through the bedroom walls.

◇◇◇

"Doctor, the eye is falling to disconnect."

"We must keep trying. She needs to wake up."

◇◇◇

A faint cry can be heard through the walls.

"Samantha?!"

A mother knows her daughter's cries. Rushing to my feet, I begin running through the corridor, which is narrow, never-ending, and covered in white walls and floors. All signs of furniture have vanished, along with my sanity. I continue running, feeling a wave of anxiety creep over me.

I hear Mike's whisper.

It's all been a lie, Jenny. Your life is a lie, Jenny.

I continue running to reach my daughter's bedroom, trying to sway my thoughts away, only for my eyes to begin blinking rapidly, almost in a deliberate attempt to block my vision. I notice her bedroom door by the end of the barren void I find myself in and push myself to reach it, all the while finding myself rapidly entering and exiting darkness.

With my vision now submerged in static and a throbbing sharp pain in my head, I fall to my knees.

My head is now weighed down by gravity. I turn to the side and watch as the door fades away slowly into the pale abyss, along with the sense of everything I've ever come to know.

◇◇◇

"I think we can disconnect it, Doctor."

◇◇◇

One last electrical surge causes my body to elevate itself off the ground. I feel something clamp onto the skin on my forehead and tug on it. The sensation of the deadly shock is too much to bear.

I scream myself into darkness.

Night Gone Weary

My breathing sounds raspy and rough, almost like it's not coming from my own chest. Startled, I open my eyes. I'm surrounded by darkness. There's nothing there. I begin to panic, wondering if I'm still asleep or not. My pulse begins to echo in my head, as loud as a drum. I sit upright, feeling myself tip slightly over the bed. As I blink my eyes slightly, I could just about make out a shape within the darkness. The more I blink, the more it appears. I turn my head towards the side of the room to try and recall where I am. I can't.

Frozen in fear, I sit in silence, as the shape in front of me becomes more visible. It was wearing a white mask, like the kind you would find at a party shop. Its eyes were hollow, it wore a still and lifeless expression. I look downwards, and notice a thin, silk black robe attached to the bottom of the mask.

The drumbeat in my head increases, as I begin to sweat. I open my mouth to scream but no sound leaves my mouth. The masked presence makes its way towards me, tilting its face sideways.

25

I feel my whole body shake in fear. The mask hovers above my bed, the end of its black robe touching the tip of my blanket.

The unfamiliar breathing that had woken me up returns. I soon realise, it was coming from the masked presence. I watch with widened eyes as the mask leans towards me, its cold hard surface now centimetres away from my face. I lean my head back slowly on the headboard of my bed, trying to escape from the mask's hypnotic gaze. Its empty eyes remain fixed onto my every movement. I shut my eyes tightly, while feeling the coldness of the mask on my cheek. "It's not real." I mutter under my breath as I grip the blanket tightly.

"Hello."

The whisper of a little girl echoes through my ears. I gasp, opening my eyes. The mask is now standing within the corner. I watch in horror as it tilts its face slightly, while the sound of a little girl's laughter appears from inside the mask.

I lay my head on my pillow, wondering when the mask would disappear. How long is it going to stand there, taunting me?

"Hi."

I hear another whisper, this time belonging to a boy. My body jolts upwards as I start to hyperventilate. The mask disappears, yet the little girl's laughter continues. My mind feels like fragmented pieces of glass. I'm falling into a dark place, trapped with the whispers for eternity.

At last, I let out a loud scream, feeling petrified to my core. My vision becomes blurred by my tears. As the walls around me start moving closer together, my perception of reality becomes warped.

I can't tell what's real and what's not anymore. My mother rushes into the room, embracing me tightly.

"It's just your medication, sweetheart."

A Night Out with the Broskis

Hey. The name's P.A.U.L, (an acronym for the words psychological assessment on units that are living.) Actually, it's PROJECT NO.56053, but you can call me 'Paul'. It's after work and I'm on a mission with my guys, my dudes, my bros, my flesh-bags with beating hearts. They're all man and no brain, trust me, I scanned them. We're on a mission tonight to get 'some'? I believe that is what the guy's say? In the line-up, we've got Greg, who resides by my- wait, let me get less 'mechanical' here.

WARNING: SYSTEM UPDATING.

UPDATING IN PROGRESS...

...

UPDATE SUCCESSFUL. HAVE A NICE DAY, PAUL.

Where was I? Oh yeah, got my hombre Greg sitting next to me, then Dylan and Ben. They're chugging down a few glasses of Mama Tamala's home brewed beer, brought straight from Nebraska. No clue how it tastes.

The guys start howling at the female specimens that walk on by. At the same time, the crowd behind me of androids and humans dance to music from the 2020's.

Their heads are wired into large headsets which connect their brains to a virtual playlist in the cloud, which is stored above them. For some reason, there's this female leaning on my shoulder. She has her chest on parade and keeps giggling at everything I say. I'm not even trying to be funny; I swear. I don't even have that function.

Greg hisses into my ear. He's nearly falling over from all the alcohol he's consuming.

"What're you doing, man?!"

I turn to my red-cheeked friend, confused.

"What do you mean?"

"The stripper's waiting for you. Go *get some.*"

"Go…get what? My purpose is to file taxes for a living."

Dylan chimes in with some incomprehensible jargon while slamming his glass of beer onto the table, with such force that it shatters in his hands.

29

In less than a second, Ben roars with laughter at Dylan's pain while he's too drunk to notice the puddle of blood beneath his hand.

Greg, meanwhile, is preoccupied with stalking the half-covered female that brings more beers to our table.

And I was made to assess these dumb dying species, was I?

While the guys continue their drunken escapades, the woman beside me leans closer and whispers into my ear.

"You're hot, you know that?~"

I look at her, perplexed. I try to scan her emotions with no luck. The only thing that successfully scans is her intoxication level. You can imagine how high it is. She leaps onto my lap and ruffles my hair with her pale, slender hands.

"I've never *done it* with an android before, darl'."

With the cogs in my head turning, I scan my electronic dictionary for the words. No data available.

30

I turn to the guys, thinking perhaps they can help me figure out this temptress's puzzle. I notice Dylan nudging Ben on the shoulder.

They wave their eyebrows at me. Greg returns from his romantic endeavours and slings his arm around my shoulder, yet again.

"This is Paul. He files women like taxes," Greg mumbles drunkenly.

He cradles yet another beer in his hand. The woman lets out a coy laugh while grabbing onto my shirt and winks at me. She begins to pull me away from the table. I look back only to hear the guys cheering for me.

I do not understand why the drunken imbeciles are cheering for me while I am being taken from them.

I'm led away from the blaring music into a room with floral design covering the walls and tranquil music playing in the background. I remember to hand the woman the $20 note that Greg left in my pocket at the start of the night.

She tucks the note into her chest area and begins taking off her shoes in a sultry manner.

"Does this turn you on, you *sexy* walking microwave?"

"Well, I suppose I'm already turned on as I have no off switch."

"*I'll* find that switch for you~"

She growls flirtatiously and proceeds to lift off my shirt. I blink, only for her body to contort and transform into a large grey filing cabinet with protruding cylinder legs and arms.

 I'd recognise that cabinet anywhere. This fine appliance is my partner at work. While I file taxes, she stamps the files and *oh, does she stamp them like an absolute warrior goddess. She sure gets my motor running whenever she's near me.*

"It's…*you*."

"Hello, Paul~"

"I-I have always admired you, Annie."

32

She silences my vocal box by placing her *narrow, smooth, thin, fibre-filled, organic, e…eco-f…friendly* receipt label on my communicator pads. Annie takes out her wire from her back compartment. She grasps her wire and begins spinning it in a scandalous manner. I am too mesmerised by her sheer beauty and boldness to look away. Her wire is long and thick, slender and very…*very*…flexible.

I have dreamt of seeing her wire, but to think she would present it so quickly towards me. There must be an established conn- ERROR.

SYSTEM ERROR.

UPDATE IN PROGRESS.

LOADING…LOADING…

HUMAN VOCAL PATTERNS AND DIALECT HAS NOW BEEN UPDATED.

As I was saying, she 'wants me' so badly.

That's good to know 'cause I wanna get so…sooo into her ' cabinets' if you know what I mean.

33

She blinks her viewfinders at me. My motor

begins humming.

"Paul, may we… *connect~?*"

 "Y…Yeah! A-absolutely!"

CW: Contains depictions of the consumption of raw meat, graphicly detailed gore, possession & cannibalism.

Mama's Warning

"Carter, how many times have I told you to stop leaving your shoes around the house?!"

As usual, my son says nothin' and slams his bedroom door shut. I'm left to pick up after his mess. He's really startin' to get on my nerves. Not only him, but the fact that my husband Tony never comes home after work an' on the rare occasion that he does, he's too tired to pay me any attention. The phone cord begins strainin' on the corner of the wall, so I stay in the kitchen.

"You need to put your foot down with Carter, sweetie, or else he's gonna continue being a disrespectful little turd to you."

Leaning on the counter while fetching a cigarette from my secret drawer, I light the stick ablaze before twirlin' the phone cord with my fingers.

"I think he misses not having his dad around, which is why he does what he does...but Pauline, he damn well knows how h-hard it is for me..."

35

I 'ear my voice begin to crack while barely holdin' onto my composure. Black dots cascade my vision as my mascara drips downwards from my eyes, stainin' my new apron.

"Oh, Lord!"

"Cassidy? Everythin' alright, hun?"

My breath shakes down the end of the line. I feel the room closin' in on me and start gaspin' for air as my throat suddenly closes.

"Cassidy, darlin', breathe, okay? Breathe. No man or son for that matter, is worth makin' you feel this way."

Pauline's words become like faint whispers as I find myself crouched down on the floor, cowerin'.

"Stop it, darl', this ain't right for ya."

I'm a whimperin'mess on the other side of the line. *Thank The Lord for them cable phones.*

"Now listen ere', you're already working your keister off looking after Mary-Lou and all that, so Carter needs to realise this and be the man of the house in Tony's place, ain't that right?"

My heavy breathin' clouds the line.

"I said, ain't that right, Cassidy?"

She repeats 'erself a lot slower and firmer. It's enough to bring me back to my senses and assist me in formin' some proper words.

"I-I can't go on like this, Pauline, i-it's just too damn-"

"Darlin', I agree, that's why you gotta be harder on the boy."

"B-But he's scared of his sister, and 'course, with his daddy ain't around-"

"The boy's father ain't dead, he's just an ass. Now you go tell that boy what's what!"

"A-Alright."

"Alright now, I'll talk to you soon, darl."

As the line goes dead, the alarm by my counter starts ringin'. Pauline's damn right. It's about time that Carter starts payin' me respect. Since his father doesn't give a flyin' turkey about his kids, it's up to me to play both good-cop and bad cop. *But right now, I need to stick to my schedule.*

37

I remember to unlock my daughter's bedroom door so I don't 'ave to kick it open with my foot while I carry her tubes in. Back in the kitchen, I rummage through the cupboards to prepare Mary-Lou's feeding tubes.

I begin cuttin' strips of raw veal and mushin' it up, just enough so it'll go down her feeder, when suddenly I 'ear bangin' comin' from Carter's bedroom walls. The ruckus is so loud that the picture frames around me begin shakin'. I put down my knife, take off my gloves and sigh, while rubbin' my temple. Enough is damn well enough.

Lord, give me strength.

With all my patience lost, I drop my daughter's feeder onto the counter without hesitation. I whip off my apron and chuck it to the floor. Pauline's words echo in my mind.

Now, tell that boy what's what.

Without any explanation needed, I slam my son's bedroom door open only to find him slammin' onto the walls with his fists while hollerin' like some kind of crazy person. I didn't raise no animal, no Lord, I did not.

"Carter Lee Jones, what in The Lord's name do you think you're doin'?!"

"I hate you, mama! You suck!"

He continues bangin' on the walls while hollerin' his taunts at me. Feelin' my anger fester through my chest, I run up to him and grab him by the wrists.

"Now, you stop that right now, you 'ear me?!"

"No! All you do is care about 'er! Everythin' changed when she was born! I hate you both!"

He squirms in my arms to try and free himself.

"The feeling's damn mutual, Carter!"

The banging comes to a stop. My son stares at me in surprise, then quickly frees himself from my grasp. Without saying anythin' more, he runs out of the door, slammin' it behind him. He turns the lock.

"Carter! Open this damn door!"

"No! Why should I?!"

"'Cuz your sister needs her feedin', now open this door!"

"No! She don't even move, watch, I'll prove it!"

I fiddle with the doorknob, but the door doesn't wanna budge. The lock's bein' as stubborn as my son.

"Carter! Open this door right now!"

I'm kicking the door while tryin' to jiggle the damn doorknob to loosen the lock.

"When I get out of 'ere, you're as good as dead, Carter Lee Jones, you 'ear me?!"

But my son ignores my cries of pleadin'. I 'ear his footsteps make his way towards where his sister's room is. That's when it hits me yet again that Mary Lou hasn't 'ad her feedin' yet.

"Carter! Don't you go in there!"

But I get nothin' but a door hinge squeakin' shut.

Then…radio silence.

The only sound I can 'ear is my own breath which gets faster the more I listen to that damn silence.

I know the bangin's stopped, but I'd rather 'ave that then dread to think what's happenin' to my little boy. *Now stop that right now, Cassidy, you 'ear? All's well. He's probably with his sister, just sat in the corner to prove a point to me. It's fine...I'm not worried. He won't do anything stupid, right?*

There's a slight gap under my son's door, all lit up by the sunlight's rays. I look through it, tryin' to peek at my daughter's door opposite my son's bedroom. Noticin; his little red shoes with the white shoelaces left by the door, my heart begins to sink. That's when I 'ear it.

"Argh!"

It echoes through the walls.

"Carter!?"

My heart picks up its pace as I scramble to my feet. I'm now resortin' to usin' my nails to try and pick the lock.

Dammit, come awn!

Another scream pierces through my ears.

"Mama!"

41

Why in the Lord's name did I leave Mary-Lou's door unlocked?!

The doorknob keeps rattlin' with my every attempt. My son's cries for help are enough to set off my tears. I'm now bangin' my shoulder on the door with all my might, prayin' to the Lord that it will open.

"Carter, momma's comin'! H-hold…on!"

Somethin' cracks as my shoulder hits the surface of the wooden door for the fifth time. I wince in pain while stumblin' back onto my son's bed. Covering my now dislocated shoulder with my other hand, I lay on his Flinstone's bed cover, the one that his Me-maw got him, out of breath. Starin' at his cartoon covered wallpaper, my eyes slowly start closin'.

The world around me begins to fade away. Small towner Cassidy just had the love of her life Tony promise her the world.

She's gleamin' under the lights of Paris. Have that dream, darl'. Enjoy one false promise after another, 'cause the only 'world' that you're gettin', is a no-good husband who spends most of his time away from home gamblin' and playin' backseat bingo with a bunch o' floozies.

"Ah! She's got my leg! M-Mama!"

I open my eyes sharply, risin' to my feet.

My baby needs me!

Rushin' over to the door, I start kickin' it down with all the strength I have left in me.

Atta girl, Cassidy! Harder!

"M-Mama! Mary Lou's hurtin' me!"

My heart continues breakin' as my boy's cries only get louder. I lean by the door, tryin' to desperately catch my breath. I feel my feet become lighter but continue standin' through the sheer determination of needin' to save my son. The words I thought I'd never say finally come out n' all.

THIS BOOK JUST MIGHT BE BATS*** CRAZY

"Carter! *Fight* 'er!"

That's when I 'ear a loud screech from the room in front of me. It's followed by the same silence as before. I fall to my knees, feelin' the world around me turn numb. I crumble to the ground and run my hands through my messy hair, screamin' my baby's name. It's finally enough to worry the neighbours as I 'ear the doorbell buzz.

A lock turns in the front door.

Oh, thank you, Lord! Someone must've called Tony!

I sweep up my words as soon as I 'ear who's there.

"Cassidy, y'all alright? I heard somethin' and thought I'd come over and check things."

It's my neighbour Greg with the spare key who calls out to me from my front porch.

Pressin' myself behind the door for him to 'ear me better, I yell from the top of my lungs while shakin'.

"Greg! Oh, Greg! I'm locked in Carter's room! Hurry!"

I 'ear footsteps rush over to the door. At last, the lock on my son's doorknob turns counter clockwise.

44

As the door opens, I waste no time in stumblin' out of the room to my feet and sprintin' towards the door in front of me.

"Cassidy, woah there! What's-"

Greg's voice turns to a whisper as I enter the room to find pools of blood splattered across my daughter's black walls. At this point, I wanna shut my eyes, but the pure terror that overtakes me, forces me to keep 'em open.

With my breath shakin', I let out a whimper.

"C-Carter?!"

Somethin' soft falls from above the ceiling, startlin' me and blockin' my path. The thing is red and pulsates in front of me. I step back, scared stiff to my stomach at what I'm seein', only to step on a long, transparent, tube, which oozes yellow liquid out of its centre.

That's when I look up. There, hang the remains of what Carter's body, torn to shreds, paradin' on the ceiling lamp like some kinda twisted paintin', while his bones and organs are free-fallin' from above.

N-no…it…can't b-be…,my sweet b-baby b-boy…

I feel my stomach go all woozy and cover my mouth while fallin' to my knees, only to fall into a pile of his squashed organs lookin' like Mrs Mrytle's Ground Beef. I reach out towards my son's blood and watch it slip through my fingers. My little girl's surrounded by the raining organs. She stares at the pulsatin' one in front of her. 'er doll-like pupils. gone, now replaced with what I'd call The Devil's darkness.

She lets out a growl. The area where her sweet tiny baby teeth used to be, now 'ave tall, wide and thorny spikes comin' outta the root of her mouth. 'er tongue, belonging to The Devil's serpent itself.

She sits in front of me, slurpin' on the blood that I'm now sittin' in. Low, dog-like growls come outta her mouth followed by her hands and legs goin' off in different directions. Her head shakes and snaps backwards. It rests on her back, while the empty holes in her eyes are soaked with the blood of my son. I watch the thing while praying to The Good Lord to save me. The more liquid she consumes from the floor, the more she moves around all possessed like.

.

"H-how could you do this?!"

 No response.

Lord...please forgive me for what I'm 'bout to do.

Picking myself up in a flurry of rage and shock, I waste no time in grabbin' my daughter by her throat.

"Why would you do this to your brother!?"

As tears fall down my eyes and my blood boils with the most anger I've ever felt, my daughter moves for the first time ever in her life in my hands. She opens her mouth, revealin' a snake-like tongue/ She runs it across my face, only to start spewin' words of darkness at me.

"H-h-u-u-n–n-g-g-r-r-y-y!"

"Y-you're no child of mine!"

The blood on my hands causes my daughter's neck to slip from my grip and fall in front of me. I watch 'er reach out towards Carter's still beating heart in front of 'er.

"M-Mary Lou! Don't y-you d-dare!"

Not carin' 'bout my words, the girl helps 'erself to the last alive remains of my baby right in front of me.

47

I watch the blood from his pumpin' arteries trickle outta 'er mouth and how the tendons of his muscles get stuck between 'er teeth with each bite taken outta it.

Greg, meanwhile, is fiddlin' with my front doorknob. He soon unlocks it and makes a runner for the front door while screamin' out to the rest of the world.

"Your kid is damned!"

Dango

You're young; it's summer. You venture out into the garden to try and get your mind off things. The corner of your eye passes his kennel. Your heart cries out in agony. A shower of memories floods your vision as you remember your dearest puppy. How you both would play with each other, comfort each other.

So, you take a step towards Dango's kennel. You haven't done so ever since his disappearance last year. You feel something crunch under the surface of your flip-flop. *W-why does it look like the snout of a sleeping fox?!* Startled, you rush inside to tell your mum, who is unfazed by this? She tells you to bring her your dad's shovel. You ask her why, only for her to reply she has unfinished business. A little later you go upstairs to play in your room, only to disregard your dolls after a while. Metallic banging noises can be heard from below.

That sounds much more interesting than roleplaying the same old royal wedding proposal with your dolls, you think to yourself.

49

You watch from your window as your mum, with her back turned to you, picks up the sleeping fox with gloves and shoves it into a rubbish bag.

Thoughts of the fox's actions suddenly seep into your mind. It was sleeping, wasn't it? Yet, its stomach was flat. Why didn't you see its stomach rising and falling with its snores? Was it actually asleep? Why did you find its snout under your flip flop? You take a moment to ponder, focusing your thoughts on the shape of its snout.

It was flat and indented. The fur surrounding it was striped, not orange. Hold on, you think. Why would a fox's fur not be orange? How can it be striped? Your neighbour's cat Clover was also striped. oh, how much you loved that cat. She used to play nicely with Dango. They were both your best friends.

You think back to how they both disappeared around the same time which led to the missing posters that went up, that your mum eventually took down. Thirty minutes later, your mum walks back into the house. You stay in your room. You recall how distant you've become from your mum since Dango's disappearance.

50

She never liked that dog. She would always watch as you would lay on the grass beside Dango, sharing imaginative stories with him. Stories you would never share with her. You think the fun would last forever.

It's the day that now pains your heart. Dango is nowhere to be seen. You search high and low for your little puppy but can't locate him. Your bottom lip begins to quiver. At that same time, from outside you can hear your neighbour Benjamin crying behind the fence. It turns out that his cat Clover has disappeared! You both cry together as a way of comforting each other. You're both only ten years old after all.

After you spend about forty-five minutes of crying, you rush back inside to tell your mum the news about Dango but she's not in the house.

You run around trying to find her, only to instead be greeted with written words of apologies near the fridge. She's gone out for the day due to work things. How could she?! Your best friend is missing, and your mum decides to go out now of all times?! —Your fist slowly clenches.

You brush the memories of the previous summer away. You're home alone again, so fearing the worst, you

51

call the police. Later, your house is soon swarmed by police cars. You hear a knock on the door and go to open it. Standing before you is your mum.

Unable to hold back your fright, you burst into tears. Mum, I'm scared, and you left to work exactly like last time! how could you leave me alone again, you wail. In response to you, she tuts and rolls her eyes.

Please step away from her, dear, says a policewoman as she softly stands between you both. You nod and take a moment to compose yourself, only to realise that your mum is in fact handcuffed. Looking down, you notice her hands covered in blood. The crimson droplets deal great damage to the wooden floor beneath your feet.

W-why is there so much blood?!

What's going on, you cry, as your pupils slowly dilate in fear. Another police officer squeezes past the conundrum by the door and escorts you to the other room.

You watch him kneel towards you and hand you a tissue from his pocket. Think you might need this; he replies in a calm voice.

***

A few hours have passed. Everything makes sense now, although you're not sure what to make of that sense anymore. With your blood boiling and glass heart shattering, you make your way back to the living room.

Your mum remains by the door, but her demeanour has changed. Instead of arrogance, guilt is plastered onto her face. It doesn't affect you in the slightest because you now realise it's as fake as her.

The intercom over the policewoman's shoulder announces that at last she has 'the pet killer' in custody.

There it is...the truth.

Never would you think that your mum would be capable of hurting you in such a way, let alone committing such a crime. You thought all these years that she loved you.

It's a few minutes later. As your mum is escorted to the police car, you rip off the Band-Aid of emotional turmoil. How could you do this to me, I hate you; I hope you rot in jail; you hear yourself screech through your overflowing tears.

The darkness is soon illuminated in blue and red flashes. With clenched teeth, you shut the door. You turn the knob locking the world away. She's no mum of yours now. After all that she has done, how she has made you and Benjamin suffer.

She must be punished. She must…for Dango's sake.

You crumble to the floor, for Dango's sake.

The J. A. C. K

I have arrived within the vicinity of the most vulnerable specimen. The levels of oxytocin suffocating the air is enough to penetrate through my flippers. This is before contaminating the species. What awaits me once I have seized control of the fleshy vessel?

It's quite disgusting to look at. It has flippers which protrude outwards and bend. It is missing the ever so important amount of seven thousand eyes for visual and hearing aid. It is missing a stem at the end of its flippers. I cannot register how this creature cannot float without a set of fangs that move upwards and downwards its back. *Just how does this creature manage the need to not fly?*

I have one purpose and one purpose only. To infiltrate the flesh covered skeleton and use it as a safe space for my hatchlings.

They must be hatched.

55

It is what The Mother ordered.

I will serve The Mother as it is my purpose.

*

I approach the specimen. While it has the back of it turned from me, I float downwards onto a soft terrain towards the thing that it is communicating into.

I gently press my fur into the object, my fibres stretching outwards, my hind claws extending. I cannot feel the process happening, as I am more drawn towards a square object that alerted all seven thousand of my eyeballs.

A tall and mentally physique specimen appears within a metallic square window. It remains frozen. It has vocal orifices curving upwards. Beside said creature on the right, I locate the thing which I wish to board.

It has sulphuric strands tied around the vicinity of the other specimen's flipper. The specimen who resides on the left now has the attachment of my blinking sockets. I quickly close my eye holes as the specimen releases me into the air. I am now within my ship's grasp. I must make haste with gaining control. As I am about to make my way into the creature's tunnel, I notice the beast turn back. I have enough of an opening to make it into the hole without interruption or risk of failing.

56

Once I land to my required destination, I find my way past the uneven terrain, past the vast array of lights which dangle from above, only then to reach my target. Its cerebral cortex.

Once I arrive there, my hind legs detach from the sides towards below me and carry me to the centre of the cerebrum. Before even being able to comprehend the magic of the specimen I now find myself in, my sockets become indulged in the mind of the creature. I soon find myself left senseless yet driven by a desire towards the second creature. I am able to obtain the sensations to see and feel what draws my vessel towards it.

It is called a 'J.A.C.K'. It is a male species.

The 'J.A.C.K' is warm when around the specimen I embody.

It will be perfect for the hatchlings.

In that moment, my thoughts are interrupted by the physical physique of the creature, the way his flippers are presented, the way his oil composited fur flows through the carbon dioxide diluted air that these specimens inhabit.

57

His voice region shines through the mind of this vessel. It is pleasing to me.

The vocal fluctuations of the male specimen amuse me.

I now plan to not only incubate the hatchlings with his assistance, but also devour him whole. Where I am from, our planet shows desire for one another by consuming the other half. That was before the war of Humoli. The devastation turned the planet into thin air. I am the last of the nooles.

The Mother was the provider of energy for us nooles as a collective. The collective was a very valuable and relevant source of energy. It was always pleasurable to spend waking hours with other nooles.

Before the war, I served The Mother, bringing it the blood of virgins through flesh vessels in order to sustain its lifeforce. I did this by teleporting the hormones to and from wherever they resided, through entering their minds and forcing them to climb aboard the neurotransmitter at a specific location depending on where they would prosper in their accommodations. The hormone of arousal is what fed our civilization.

The nooles are no more.

I will avenge The Mother.

I will repopulate my people and planet.

*

"I'm telling you Clair, lowkey, I think I'm in love! ~"

"Shut. Up. No way did Jack ask you out!"

"He totally did!"

"No way!"

"Way!"

The anticipation of the specimen's arousal looms through the air. It's got an alluring taste to it, too interesting to pass through without getting a taste for myself. With my hind legs, I slowly pierce myself into the fleshy, uneven terrain below. That is when I find myself corroded by odours. I follow the odours through the mind of my vessel.

"Jack's so hot!"

By steadying my hindlegs, I pierce further into the flesh. I guide the specimen to an outing. My surroundings fill with the scent of Oestrogen and Testosterone.

I manoeuvre my vessel to the familiar creature within its mind. The creature is that of my own, full of Oestrogen.

The two specimen's communicate, to which I allow as I have hopes of the J.A.C.K. to appear. He must appear for my plan to go accordingly.

"Jack sounds so tasty, Clair!"

More.

"Mm mm mmm, he's *such* a snack!"

Further. I must obtain the vocal patterns of this creature.

"OMG, don't panic but *look* at who just showed up!"

"Hey girls, where's the party at?"

That is when the specimen of my own personal desires appears in front of my new vessel. I find myself drawn towards the J.A.C.K as my eye sockets attach to him.

Its uranium infused vision aids make decent towards

60

the creature I inhabit, until my vessel has now been transported into his arms by a collision from the other oestrogen filled creature that is familiar within the mind of my vessel.

That is when I press my hind legs to the core of the vessel's uneven terrain. It makes the structure of the vessel begin to shake. This uranium filled vessel has the perfect incubation chamber for the hatchlings.

This will be substantial enough.

"Hey, Jack ~"

"Abbs, damn, you're looking *good.*"

I do my best to remain attached to the flesh. As I begin to push each of my eggs into the centre of my new vessel, I manage to gain control of the vocal regulator.

"Good enough to *eat*, perhaps~?"

Upon my command, I guide the vessel's vocal regulator to the J.A.C.K's vocal regulator. The specimen is taken aback but there is vocalisation of the hormone replacement eggs working. The two vessels collide, releasing oxytocin, serotonin and pheromones into the air produced by the vessel and the J.A.C.K.

61

Using the other sets of legs that I possess; I climb into the core of the terrain. That is when I am able to pass the fleshy exterior and descend downwards into the vessel's main source of power. It is a pulsating, flesh coated substance. I am drawn to it more than the vessel who is intertwining with my own within the moment. One moment of extraction is all it takes. I turn myself spherical as fangs begin protruding from my fur. Within seconds of penetration, the artery begins to resemble the uranium I encountered earlier.

"Mmm, Jack, I could just eat you up~…"

"Oh yeah? Well then…*what's stopping you*?~"

That's exactly that.

Nothing will be able to terminate the transformation from happening at this point.

Nothing at all.

My view is soon obscured by the tendrils of the specimen grasping its core area of intel centre of information.

"God, no! W-what the hell did I jus-?! I-I totally didn't mean to say that!"

62

The specimen begins to move in a swaying motion that is not being orchestrated by any means of my forced control.

"Woah, Abbs, you don't look so good. I'll go get you some water."

The J.A.C.K. disappears from my vessel's field of view, only to teleport back with a rotund material that contains clear liquid inside of it. J.A.C.K holds it up to my vessel's vocal communicator and makes contact with the vertebral column. Round patterns are produced upon the coated flesh of my vessel by the J.A.C.K

It seems a connection is becoming established. I will succeed in bringing back The Mother. In time, this vessel shall become The new Mother of the nooles.

I will obtain full control of this vessel…all in good time.

Author's Note: The following individual characters in this story are consenting young adults.

CW: contains light sexual imagery as well as implied cannibalism and body horror.

My Sweet Cephalothorax

He feels so good that I can't stop myself. The way his body moves against mine, the way his hands know exactly where they need to go, what they need to touch. His hot breath is against my ear. His whisper, like a match igniting a flame within me. He continues teasing me, whispering promises while his lips softly travel downwards my neck. A soft moan escapes my lips. He smirks.

"J-Jack, the m-movie-"

"What about it?"

He speaks with a husky voice while nibbling on my earlobe. I look up and see the sky. It's a blanket of darkness submerged in a thousand lights. I hear the screams of sorority girls from the speakers of the drive-in cinema as the back seat of his car envelops me further

. He pushes me into the back door and climbs on top of me, pressing his chest against mine, pinning my arms above my head against the window.

I can't lose control…I can't!

64

His eyes meet mine. They speak a thousand words. I can barely look away, captivated by his baby blues which have the glint of the moonlight bouncing off them.

The way he looks at me…

I feel myself getting hotter and more desiring for his touch as his knee rubs in between my legs.

Finally, after repressing myself for two years, I now find myself about to go all the way with the love of my life. Jack has never judged me about anything. He has always been there for me…and tonight, it's my turn to show him just how much I appreciate that.

He nods at me slowly, before taking off my top. The cold kiss of the evening breeze makes me shiver. His warm breath creeps over the shell of my ear.

As I blink, I suddenly find Jack muffled, crying for help.

N-no…I-leave him alone!

Two hands shake me back to reality. Jack's eyes are filled with concern. I turn my head to the side. My eyes begin to overflow. His slender hand softly strokes my cheek.

"Abbs, you okay?"

"I-I'm scared…"

Why have we chosen him of all guys?!

"Don't be."

"But w-what if I hurt you?"

The last thing I want is to hurt Jack, but I'm not sure I can control myself. The way he lays on top of me, the closeness of him. I want one thing and one thing only – to come home and wash his sweat off my body. No. we need his warmth and his love, to trap him in our web, so he never leaves you!

B-Be quiet!

He must incubate the hatchlings.

Please, don't hurt him!

We must feed.

There's fear in my eyes as a burning sensation courses through my ribs. In that moment, the feeling of a thousand knives stab through my flesh as the frame of my spine begins to crack and contort into a curved position.

Biting down on my lip to keep myself from screaming, I taste blood. Tears begin trickling down my face as I wince. I begin to sweat, feeling prickles against my skin, and this time, it's not from Jack's stubble.

It's happening, whether I like it or not.

I'm met with worried eyebrows in response. There's silence. The only sound I can hear is my own heartbeat throbbing in my head. I let out soft pants to try and distract myself from the pain. The leather seat beneath me, now damp with sweat.

Jack hovers over me, scanning my expression. His shoulders tense up. Sensing worry in him, I nod to reassure him I'm alright. Straight after, his shoulders relax. His hand resumes stroking my cheek softly yet hesitantly.

"You *know* I'd never hurt you, Abbs."

He smiles. No other words are needed.

Ignore the thoughts...focus on control!

"I-I don't think this is a good idea, Jack."

"Abby, we've waited two years."

67

My pulse increases. I feel my cheeks flare up. My legs begin to tingle in excitement. I'm left breathless for no reason. With Jack, I can forget what's happening.

I *want* to forget.

Jack's lips hover over mine. His voice overflows with desperation.

"I can't wait any longer, Abbs," he taunts in low whispers as his hand moves downwards my thigh and hovers there. I feel an electrical pulse pass through my body like a firework.

"And…I don't think *you* can either."

He's right. I can't.

I press my lips against his, finally closing the gap. I kiss him with hunger, a yearning I've never felt before. My tongue explores his mouth with intense concentration, making sure to not leave any crevices untouched. I hear him moan my name softly as our tongues rub together.

I feel a tearing sensation through my flesh, yet the bliss of Jack's tongue against mine overpowers it.

I need *more*.

My hands slide under his shirt, making sure to stroke Jack's chest in ways he only dreams of me doing so. I plant kisses alongside his neck, while his hands roam around my body, caressing the frame of my back softly. He pulls me up towards him. The force pushes him over, so I sit on top of him.

He's shirtless. He takes a moment to admire my beauty before his hand continues travelling downwards my abdomen. My core begins to ache for him.

"Abbs...I love you."

Finally, those three words.

I close my eyes. The legs I'd been carefully hiding were finally revealing themselves. I feel them spring straight out of my spine with a snap. I feel a ribbon of silk form down below.

Without warning, the legs climb onto his back. Oblivious to this, he continues to rub my core.

69

The back of my legs begins entrapping him, clamping onto his shoulders, pushing him further downwards onto the leather seat. He smirks and closes his eyes, taking in my moans of pleasure.

A knot builds up in my stomach as I feel myself reaching the edge.

"O-oh, J-Jack!"

Upon release, my skin slowly sheds off revealing six extra eyes, one set above, two below my already existing ones. I sit there, panting.

A moment of silence passes. Confused by this, Jack opens his eyes. Red eyes stare back at him. His beautiful girlfriend, now an eight-eyed demon, straddling him. As she pants, he notices the white, sharp fangs protruding from her mouth. He tries to push her off to no avail. She looks at him in confusion as her drool drips down onto his cheek.

70

"W-What the fuck?! Y-You're a monster!"

"How could you say that?! You **love me**!"

"G-Get off me!"

He whimpers under me, while struggling to reach for the door handle.

"Come…on…,oh s-shit!"

My hind legs hover above his face. I bring his face close to mine. My fangs extend themselves.

*"*Jack, it's me, your **A-b-b-y-b-e-a-r**."

He shakes his head violently as I blink at him. There are tears in his eyes. He closes them tightly, continuing to whimper. I hear a loud growl come out of my mouth.

What is this rage I feel growing within me?! It's telling me to, to…to **make him p-a-y-!**

"W-why can't you l-o-o-k- at me?!"

He screams in agony as my fangs pierce through his eye sockets, hooking onto the flesh surrounding his eyeballs.

"You're meant to *love* me!"

71

My web down below thickens. I want to stop myself, but I can't.

A Fool in Knight's Armour

"My darling, now we shall seal our engagement with a kiss," I cheerfully quip while facing my beloved with a gaze as warm as the sun beaming downwards onto a long, clear stream of water.

"Now, now, Frederic, you will first have to catch me in order to receive your kiss ~," my fiancé replies as she places her hand softly upon my cheek and leans in slowly towards me, only to pull back at the last minute and rise to her feet from the picnic blanket we lay upon. I lay in confusion as my dearest lets out a heavenly laugh while dusting a few blades of grass that attack her dress. She disappears into the back of the garden. I quickly jolt to my feet, grinning while following her direction, only to hear deafening silence in return.

I soon find her body upon the cobblestones. The stream of clear blue water is mixed in with the fresh crimson droplets which fall from the bottom of her now torn dress. Her eyes lay open. I kneel towards her, embracing her cold body.

73

It's there that I notice the bleeding out wounds that poisons her body, a dagger lies pierced straight through her heart. It appears silver and features an incomprehensible crest.

"D…Darling?" I reply whilst trembling.

I grit my teeth until I taste my own blood. Abigail. My dear Abigail. Struck down in less than a minute.

As I kneel, now drenched in my fiancé's own blood, I begin to lose all my composure and slowly contort into a ball-like shape, pressing my face into her bosom, where I sob loudly, - the loudest of which a knight such as I have ever done so. With my face covered in her remains, I stop myself from buckling to my knees even further. If she saw what I've become because of her death, oh, how she would pity the fool she was to marry.

As nightfall passes, I scoop the corpse of my beloved in my arms and make haste to the castle. My trusty steed Thompson rushes through the trees while the sun is just on the peak of the horizon. A cold breeze passes me, causing Thompson to halt in fear.

"M-Mind Abigail, you f-foolish, wretched steed!"

74

Clutching onto my fiancé's body, I soon notice a faint golden shimmer around her neck. I examine the object closer with care. It's a pendant, as golden as the king's riches.

How it got upon her neck, I haven't the slightest clue. Turning over the pendant gently reveals the initial 'R' engraved to the back of it.

Where exactly did this pendant come from? Perhaps her father might know.

Without dallying in my thoughts, I continue making my way towards the castle. Upon arriving, I quickly strip myself of my blood stained top and cover my fiancé's body with the picnic blanket, then leave my horse by the castle gates. It is not every day that a knight brings their future in-law home the corpse of his murdered daughter. I can be hanged for treason if I am not careful in how I approach this to his majesty.

Perhaps I best leave word of my fiance's death unspoken.

As I'm soon ushered into his throne room, he offers me some salutations in the form of beverages, to which I politely decline. He seems paler than usual and slightly disoriented.

"Come my boy, for you have bought me quite the bounty of a Dragon upon your questing, I see! A little diminutive in size however I shall accept your gift of the wretched beast's offspring! Huzzah!"

Upon seeing his current state, I clear my throat and quietly place the covered body behind the settee out of his way, only for the king to begin asking how his daughter is doing, while stumbling on his words in certain moments. As I am about to bring myself to answer his question with the truth broken up softly, I notice how he loosens the collar of his cape nervously.

***

As the sun bids farewell to the skies of yesterday, His Majesty summons me to his study bedrooms and displays in the open a book titled 'family history'.

He begins a backstory of when he was just a poor boy, alone in the street.

I sit and politely absorb his tales, all the while keeping a steady eye on the covered body behind the settee. After his tales cease to an end, I clear my throat, showering him with light applause.

"Your Majesty, may I enquire about something?"

The image of my fiancé's limp corpse looms over my mind.

"Y...yes, what is it, my son?"

I pause, trying to focus my thoughts onto the correct wording.

"Do you... perhaps possess any acknowledgement within the kingdom of people who carry the initial 'R' within their birth name?"

77

The king's face suddenly falls into an expression of dejection and rage, as he slams his golden chalice with a mighty force onto the side of his throne, spilling some of the salutations in the process onto his nightly attire.

Flinching, I continue.

"With the recent law you enforced on the letter itself, and all-"

"Do *not* speak of that letter to me, ever!"

The king's eyes grow heavy with guilt and despair. I stop inquiring and get up to leave,only for the floorboard beneath me to crack inwards itself, revealing what looks to be a flower laced journal. While his majesty is occupied with drowning his sorrows in intoxication, I sneak the journal behind my back and disappear to my own chambers, discarding Abigail's corpse with her father. The King begins wailing into his chalice as I leave.

It's there that I take to my chamber and glide through the journal. I discover Abigail's handwriting scribed across each page so delicately upon letters addressed to someone who goes by the initial 'R'.

78

I continue reading onwards and find my blood beginning to boil.

'After Frederic's date, I shall be alone. Come for me! It is there that we will run away together, free from everything! Frederic may be a knight, but naught is he the keeper of my heart.'

A loose note by my foot reads: 'Father knows all! He found out that I love another, who is already wed himself. I am ashamed of my actions, yet naught ever ashamed of my heart's choice of you. I have nay bestowed my eyes upon my father this infuriated in me before. I have no choice but to continue as I am. No matter whom I marry, I will always love you, Richard. Return to your kindred ones. This will be my last letter to you. ~ your devoting wife, Abi.'

The journal falls to my feet as my eyelids grow heavy. The memory of my fiance, without knowing of her treachery and deceit shall simply be stored within my dreams for the remainder of my days.

79

Come dawn, I shall find shelter and accommodation elsewhere, perhaps within another kingdom. Like my deceased fiance who moved her heart and affections onto another man, I too shall move my heart towards locating a better morrow for myself.

Befriending The Tears

The water has always been there for me, ever since I could remember. I feel it flow within every fibre of my being. It soothes me in ways which affection and love cannot, for reasons unknown to me. Every day I lay upon the waves where the Earth and Heavens just about touch, look upwards and notice the bright blue sky, never changing, always as clear as a single tear, not one cloud scattered in sight. *As much as I enjoy the beauty that the view bestows upon me daily, is it so wrong of me to wish for a change?*

Still, I am not alone. As well as the clear sky, and ocean waves, I have the sun, who always greets me with a bright beam of warmth. It reflects itself above my transparent body, heating it with a whisper of light.

I like to think that the nature surrounding me is my family. The few palm trees that stand upon the sand, swishing softly in the warm breeze. They shield the seagulls which cry in excitement whenever they spot crabs along the shore.

I often find myself absorbed in the movement of the waves, as the sunlight shines upon them, morphing their reflection and shades of blue and white into horses prancing along the current. When faced with stronger winds, my tastebuds meet the saltiness of the ocean, the roughness and bitterness of grainy sand.

Tiny clear spheres suddenly begin to fall from above.

What are these things? They keep damaging the ocean by creating circular dents.

I feel strange, concerned for my beloved sky, frightened, yet no longer alone.

They continue falling, whispering to each other about how scared they feel. I sit upright, reaching outward to hold one. It feels slippery, like how water normally feels, yet also warm on the inside.

I hold it up to my face, and observe it, only to accidently have the transparent droplet slip from my grasp and slide down my water bathed limbs.

82

It lands with a 'plop' into the ocean in front of me, disappearing from my view, while letting out a tiny scream of terror.

I blink for a few seconds, tilting my head in confusion at its response.

I wonder if they all do that.

To test my theory right, I expand my body outwards, capturing a few unsuspecting tears into my grasp, who are all minding their own business, mindlessly being absorbed into the water. As I do so, the pressure of my body lifts the aquatic crystals from the water, forming tiny, star shaped tears from their remains.

I stare at the starry tears, which jiggle round with the waves. As I lean in to hold one of them, it slowly backs away from my touch.

I tilt my head softly, registering their response. The stars huddle together, transforming into one huge tear, which lay in front of me, smiling.

At last, a friend.

I Gave It Another Go

I followed the long narrow hallway to where my mum was resting. I walked into the room and took a seat on a plastic blue chair beside her bedside. I looked up, noticing the bland grey colour the wall found itself covered in, the slight cracks which were shaped like tiny lightning bolts. I noticed the many rounded lights, spread out in narrow rows which went on infinitely. On the floor, tiny splatters of blood covered my shoe. I stared at the blood, intensely, as my mind tracked back to the incident once more.

***

It was just me and mum, on our way to see the landmarks on Route 66, fourteen days of pure desert and sights to take in, which gave me more than enough time to make it up to her.

I rocked out in the driver's seat to the sweet sound of Lynyrd Skynard's vocals on blast till they suddenly came to a stop. At last mum faced me but in dead silence. The only sound I could have heard was my own heartbeat, pulsating in my head.

THIS BOOK JUST MIGHT BE BATS*** CRAZY

From the corner of my eye, I saw mum shutting the window, her reflection trying to figure out what words to say. Her blue jumper shone through the glass.

Christ. Here it comes…

"Dylan…just explain *one* little thing to me."

"Sure," I said, while maintaining my focus on the road and only the road. I gripped the leather steering wheel steadily, feeling my hands become damp.

"Why did you decide to drop out of Uni after only two days?"

"Coz, it's not for me."

I kicked my seat back and reached for the radio, only to have my hand slapped.

"Jesus, mum!"

She said nothing and looked at me with straight up disappointment in her eyes. I cleared my throat nervously and thought of how to save my skin at that moment.

"Look, I tried doing art, yeah? It didn't jam with me, so I dropped out, end of."

85

THIS BOOK JUST MIGHT BE BATS••• CRAZY

She crossed her arms.

"But I-I don't understand, I thought you loved art!" She protested.

"Yeah mum, don't get me wrong, I did for a while…but now I'm more into music, okay?"

I quickly turned my focus from the road to see her reaction. She looked at me with a confused expression plastered across her face. Realising I wasn't having any of her nagging on this holiday, she sighed in defeat and leaned her chair backwards. I turned my back and grinned like an idiot, when suddenly-

"Dyly, look out!

Out of nowhere, a wild deer had appeared in the middle of the road. My mind went numb. I tried to slam down on the breaks in time to avoid the deer, but the panic made me lose control of the steering wheel.

The car skid across the highway, screeching as the tires were stuck and firmly locked into place. Mum held onto me like a vice while her screams echoed through my ears. It was like a scene out of Final Destination.

The steering wheel spun out of control, causing the car to flip onto the side and come to a halt. I watched as the window beside mum shattered into her flesh, before my very eyes. The impact of the crash was surreal. The front of my car was dented, smashed, and smoked slightly.

It felt like my stomach had flipped itself inside out. My neck felt like it had a blade shoved through it even though I was wearing a seatbelt.

During the crash, I somehow hit my head on the dashboard from the impact and ended up with a massive red bloody dent across my forehead.

I looked over at mum, who was lying limp over the dashboard, her head lifelessly drooped over her seatbelt. Her favourite blue jumper was anything but, covered in dark stains of her own blood. Then I blacked out.

***

The second I stared at mum, my heart had sunken into my chest.. I was faced with the harshest reality of them all, as I saw her surrounded by all them wires. A long tube was connected to her mouth, which helped ventilate oxygen to her lungs. Her white gown rose with every artificial puff of breath from the machine she was hooked onto. I took her limp, pale hand into mine and rested my forehead on it.

It's all my fault this happened. I should have given Uni a shot.

"I'm s-so s…sorry, mum…p...please be okay.."

***

It's been two years since the accident. I decided to give Uni another shot, taking a degree in music. I started wearing blue. Blue shoes, blue hoodies, blue trousers. My current girlfriend thinks I'm going nuts…and maybe I am.

When I look up at that blue sky, I feel her presence. She lives on in the colour blue, in fact, it's the colour she was buried in. As long as I continue to fill my life with blue, mum can continue living.

88

My Walking Reflection

Ever since we moved to this town, I had this strange feeling that I was being watched. It left me always feeling insecure whenever I went out for walks on my own, either to walk the dog or do a supermarket run for my mum.

My friends thought I've slowly lost my mind from the move, but I know that's not the case. I wasn't able to shake off how it felt that someone was truly out to get me. One night, I stood by my bedroom window. I wanted to prove to others that there was someone out there, who lurked in the darkness.

One afternoon, I walked home from school, alone. As I made my way down the street, I heard faint footsteps from behind me. I became instantly alarmed and turned around to check. Nothing was there. As I continued walking, the footsteps grew louder. I picked up the pace, as did the footsteps.

I started running, doing my best to get away from whoever was chasing me. I ended up in a dark, narrow alleyway. I looked around frantically, there were nothing but tall shadows that phased between the darkness. The foul stench of decaying fruit made my eyes water in disgust. Dumpsters full of plastic rubbish bags surrounded me. As I walked forward, I noticed a single dumpster abandoned by the side of the wall.

I had hit a dead end.

A figure stood behind me. There was nowhere left to run. The figure approached me and grabbed my wrist before I moved. The hand belonged to a boy, late into his teens. I stared with widened eyes at him. He stared back at me.

He looked like me. How could he look like me?

"W-Who are you!?"

The boy panted as he tried to catch his breath. I noticed his eyes, how watery they became. I just stood there in silence. He wiped his tears with his sleeve and softened his grip on my wrist.

"I'm your twin brother."

WHY

The bottom of my heels clicked with every motion of my seething anger. I noticed his gaze now facing the floor, his eyes covered by his dark messy raven hair. Around us, were unpacked boxes, complimenting the vibe.

"Babe?"

As he faced me, I turned my back to him.

"Don't you dare say one word!"

"Look, you've made your point, but don't I get a chance to speak?"

"I don't want to hear your excuses!"

"If you'd just let me get a word in-"

I sharply turned my direction to him, mascara pouring from underneath my eyes. A deep sensation began to tighten within my stomach, which slowly crawled its way upwards.

Saliva started to build up at the back of my throat. I swallowed hard, trying to force it back down, to no success. Mark then got up, flashing his stupid puppy eyes at me.

91

I noticed his arm reached out to wipe my tears. My hand abruptly came into contact with his clean-shaven jawline.

"Ow! Bloody hell Beth!" he yelped, backing away from my sudden attack.

"D-Don't!" is all I managed to say.

As I gazed at him in anger, the pressure of my saliva increased. Realising that too much of it had built up, I quickly covered my mouth with my hands, which only made things worse.

There she was, painting on the floor, like a dog. She had this look on her face. Not sure what it was…but her eyes, man, her eyes screamed crazy. She coughed and retched while crying.

Then out came the phlegm. Christ, the phlegm. – fifth time this month. It went everywhere, on the counter, her clothes, the new floors. I was gonna retch from it.

So, I did what any man would do - covered my mouth with my shirt to stop myself gagging, then panicked while grabbing whatever tissue box I could find that wasn't covered in spit. Turned my back for a second, next thing I knew, she went limp.

I'm not made to deal with this shit!

My thoughts trailed back to the club last night. Marcy in that smoking dress, the way her body moved against mine. Damn, last night, I was a king. Now, I'm just a peasant, whipped by my wife's illness, standing in God knows what, after *just* moving here.

God sake, all I wanted was a shag, not another night in A & E.

My phone rang. It was Marce.

I hung up and shook my head.

Let me concentrate, Marce!

93

I stepped through the pool of fresh spit and rolled up my sleeves. I wiped the foam from her mouth, with a fistful of tissues. Another flat, another cleaner's bill.

Her hair was mixed in with the puddle of spit, so I moved it. That fiery red hair…enough to drive a man nuts, so full of life, until the illness hit, making her weaker, fatter, less fuckable.

But…I made a vow, didn't I?

"9-9-9, what's your emergency?"

"It's Mark Klien. I need an ambulance again for my wife. "

A Teenage Roadman's Guide to Love

It's Thursday and I've just got out of detention from my music teacher. I'm vexed. The drops of rain make a continuous melody as they hit the ground. It sounds rubbish. I stare at the empty entrance gate, lost in thought. My phone buzzes, knocking me back to reality. You gotta be joking…mum's running late again.

I look at my watch.

Got some time to kill. God's sake, allow this rain, fam. It's meant to be June.

I decided to head down to my favourite hangout spot just down the road from school. As soon as I take a step through those familiar double glass doors, my stress from the day instantly fades away, as the smell of crushed cocoa beans and toasted marshmallows fill my nose. I grab a drink and sink into the softness of my seat. It's quiet. *Sometimes even I gotta have some peace and quiet, you get me?*

There's nothing I like more than a quiet place to sit and think about-

Her.

95

I call her the 'coffee-shop girl'. I don't really know her name and like hell I'm okay with keeping things that way. She's got to be the most beautiful girl I've ever seen, man. The way her hair hangs over her shoulders, how the colour of her eyes reminds me of my favourite Fortnite skin.

I can't stop thinking about her. Course, there's no way she'd settle for a short, freckled, amateur guitarist like me. I know I'm in year Eight, but I got a lot to offer a girl, yeah? For starters, I'd *share* my Adidas trainers with her. It don't get any betta' than that, let me tell you.

I feel like I'm losing my mind. It's not like me to get a crush. I mean, do guys even get crushes? Don't we just, like, tell a girl if we think they're well fit without the romantic stuff? I'm telling you, there's something about this girl that makes me want to listen to my teachers in class for real and do work, even though we've never talked.

I must really like her.

Anyways, I gotta talk to her. It's today or never. To help me out, I've called on the big guns.

"Hey, man."

Right on time.

That annoying voice belongs to my g, Ben. I guess you can call him my 'hype man' as he's always in my corner and always has my back. *He's like a proper sword to my shield.* Mans kind of a big deal at school, always flirting with the older girls. They see him as some kind of good-looking prince. Dunno knows how when we're the only guys in our class can't handle seein' a frog cut up. My only guess is that being from America works out for him more than he thinks. *Ben's out here saying he knows Minecraft youtubers to get the popular girls to notice him and it's actually workin' tho, like the flirtin' game ain't playin' bro, but Ben's proper playin' the game itself, without needin' a controller and all.*

Basically, one time, Ben heard me talking to one of my other mandem about 'feelings' that guys get during puberty. I said it was for science homework.

Since then, g has wanted nothin' more than to become my wingman in helping me get the 'coffee princess' to notice me. Yeah, he gives people dumb nicknames too.

How is this guy seen as a prince? Nah, forget that. If anyone's willing to help me out, it's him.

He smacks me well hard on the back before grabbing a seat.

My back now aches like hell.

"Ow! What the hell, bruv?! Why?! Ow! Allow it, fam…tch, when did g get so strong?"

"Coach has me working out now as well as running track. Now then, where's your 'Kōhī-Hime'?" (Coffee princess)

"Bruv, first he's not 'Coach'. He's Sir. Second, don't- don't call her that."

"What's her name, then?"

I sip on my drink without saying nothin' back.

"Danny, you still don't know her name, bro?"

Not just that, I know nada about her. The only thing I know is that she orders the same hot chocolate as me: 'Cococabana Sunrise.' How'd I find that out? -

by accidently bumpin" into her one time. That's how
we met. It was a month ago.

The opposite of what my sister's romance movies
call a 'meet cute', as the girl's chocolate drink ended up
staining my new Adidas trainers. What, I needed to educate
myself, yeah?

She bowed and said somethin' in Japanese.
That's when I felt it. How could I not? She was such a peng
ting, swear down. Skin like a flower, eyes as beautiful
as...something well pretty. The best part is, she looked like
one of those six former girls.

Noice. Have I scored big time or what?

Ben notices me gazin' at her.

"Damn, is that the princess?!"

 "Shhh!"

I clamp his mouth shut with my hand as people stare
at us. I drink to shut my thoughts up. He mumbles
somethin' but mans can't understand what he's saying, you
get me? I feel somethin' wet on my hand. I give him one on
the shoulder.

"Oi! Don't lick me!"

99

He laughs it off and stands up, archin' over me, swear down he's legit built like an Enderman from Minecraft. *Pshh, n-not that I still play it coz like I'm way too old for that game for like babies and that, yeah…*

His arm wraps around my shoulders.

"Danny my man, *that*, is Aoi Takashi, she's staying with my neighbours for a bit in their B&B."

Nah, no way he's seri- h-how long has 'a bit' been?!

"Aoi…Takashi…"

"Yeah, she's hot, huh? Hey, lucky for you, I know a little Japanese."

"Nah, you don't. Come off it.."

He nudges my arm twice with his elbow.

"You little wuss. Watch this, man."

I choke on my drink. The idiot prince takes that as a sign to walk up to her. On the way there, he walks backwards, clicking his fingers while winking at me.

Oh, shit! I just remembered that the only Japanese he knows is from watching anime! Oi, wasteman! Get your anime loving arse back here before you ruin things!

100

He leans across her table, tryin' to act smooth. I watch and laugh to myself at how stupid he looks.

I hear him chuckle as they both look over to my table. I look away towards the guitar case by my feet.

You're so lucky you get to hide in there!

I hear a girl's giggle followed by footsteps comin' closer. My heart starts thumpin' under my uniform.

I feel a tap on my shoulder and jump in my seat. There she stands in all her glory. She quietly hums under her breath the sweetest melody as the sunlight from the window reflects off her peng green eyes.

"Daniel Hern, *this is* Aoi Takashi. Well, scoot over, man, *I* do believe we've got a lady next to us, ah ha~"

The idiot grins like a div while pullin' out a seat for Aoi. The girl bows, waves and smiles all cute like before taking the seat facin' us.

My eyes are glued to her. I look like that blond vampire meme from a couple of years ago. *That works out y'know, coz I want to be buried twenty miles deep into the ground right now.*

I feel my arms become sweaty. I'm so nervous I don't say shit.

101

Come on Danny, say somethin'! Anythin', bruv!

Be a man!

I wanna speak, then remember that she don't speak English so I kick Ben from under the table. He don't flinch, but smiles while one tear falls down his cheek.

My kick wasn't even that hard, bro!

He then shoots me a thumbs up, while I roll my eyes.

Ayo, don't scare me like that, g.

We sit in silence for like a minute or two. I watch Aoi take a sip of her drink. I'm busy tappin' my hand with my fingers under the table like its some kinda guitar hero drum but Aoi, yeah, she's all calm like.

Why can't I be like that?!

"Takashi-san, this is Daniel Hern."

Ben points to me as he talks. I sit there and smile and nod like them penguins from that film. Aoi nods at me.

Nice! Get in, lad!

"It's nice to meet you both."

I'm biting my cup while shuffling my chair to Ben.

"What did she say?"

"I got this, bro."

He gives me a long arse wink.

He's 'bout to get a long arse slap to go with it.

"Takashi-san, my man Danny here thinks that you're a cutie. What do you think about that?"

He taps his hand on the table, as if to be all dramatic about what he's saying. Meanwhile, my heart does one as I watch her.

What you doin' now, bruv?! This is too painful to live through. Bruv needs to pull a speedrun or somethin;.

"E-Excuse me?"

My head sways back and forth, like I'm watching a tennis-match. I stop when she looks at me, her lip all wobbling.

Why does she look uncomfortable? Rah, what's Ben been chattin'?!

103

I'm fumin' at Ben but his majesty just smirks while patting my shoulder. *If anythin', mans the majesty here and Ben's the royal clown, hah, yeah.*

"Trust the process, man."

"Allow this fam, tch, she looks like she's gonna cry!"

"In anime terms, that means she likes you~"

He wiggles his little stupid eyebrows in front of me.

I swear down if he ruins this for me, I'm gonna do him in. Ben knows I don't watch no anime but even mans over here can tell Aoi's obviously uncomfortable 'bout somethin'.

I push his face away from mine, running my hands through my hair, looking like I just lost a Fortnite match.

Aoi's fingers grab onto her cup as I catch her looking at the door. Ben's sounds like he's hackin' somethin' up his throat.

"Basically, Daniel's 'into you'."

She looks at me in a split second, yeah? tilting her head in confusion and allat'. I'm 'bout to mentally head out.

"Oi! What you saying?!" I hiss.

He faces me with his arms crossed, looking smug.

"Relax! I'm on a roll. Just been saying that you're *into her*."

He clicks his teeth.

"Mans did what?!"

I turn to her, waving my hands nervously like my sister would as soon as you mention anything to do with Harry Styles to her. She's mad for the guy.

"S-see, I-I, think you're like, f-fit?"

I decide to be a complete dumbass coz of Ben.

Ben's got his arm over my shoulder. *Bruv, I swear down, I'm not playin' games right now.*

"In fact, *he* wants to know if *you'll* go out with him ~ "

I watch her smile fade as he talks. She waves her arms nervously in front of her face, making tiny, embarrassed sounding noises.

Things are looking good! I'm getting excited, man!

105

After a few minutes, Aoi shakes her head while bowing.. I grab Ben by the collar of his jacket, looking proper mad at him.

"Oi, what did you say?!"

"Relax, you're nearly in there!"

He hits my chest again.

'Bout to break bruv's hand in a second.

"In where?!"

"Shhhh…watch the master at work."

He puts his hand on my mouth to shut me up.

Mans screwing up then he be out here trying to stop me? Nah, allow it.

I elbow him in the stomach. He shakes off my attack with a laugh. *Oi, anime fanboy, get back to scoring with Aoi for me, yeah? Stop havin' fun laughin' with me! We can laugh later bruv!*

"Daniel wants you to be his girlfriend, Takashi-san."

Aoi looks at us, and blinks slowly before getting up from her seat. We both look at her like two lost mutts. I fling Ben's hand away from my mouth and try to use sign language from television and that to say 'what's wrong?' using Ben's hands instead of mine coz I can't be arsed to elbow him again. before she could leave. She turns, no longer smilin'.

"I think you should pay your boyfriend more attention, Daniel."

As she speaks to me in English. I stare at her like a knob, captivated in proper awe like. Her voice like two diamonds bein' all shiny and pretty and stuff, like woah *even her English accent is so sweet soundin' and peng.*

Ben pulls his hands away from me quicker than a Fortnite twitch streamer realisin' they left their camera on after finishing a match.

Aoi walks away.

Ayo, I know she's leavin' and allat but she's so peng I'm gonna lose it!

"Where *is* she going, fam?!"

He's looking at his phone, so I kick his foot.

"Danny, what the heck, man?!"

107

THIS BOOK JUST MIGHT BE BATS***CRAZY

"Oi! What did she- Did-did it work? Did mans get her number?"

Ben takes some tiny little breath for someone doing jogging for P.E. and looks at me. He mumbles something in Japanese and goes as red as his mom's car.

He's fast as f off his seat.

The hell's going on?! This is the same guy that normally walks instead of runs when we get caught for selling fizzy drinks in the playground. Why is this enderman of a guy running like a new Fortnite DLC just dropped?

I shrug and faceplant my head on the table and bang my fists like some little baby man. *Don't judge me, yeah? Mans heart be hurting, aight?!*

Epic fail. Going home with a fat L. That's what I get for liking a girl way out of my league!

CW: contains depictions of light sexual content / sexual language)

Love Me Numbly

"Mm~ Oh Dyl~ Oh ye...ah...mmm. Oh, give it to me, baby~"

"Woah, Megs, easy!"

He pulls his hands away from my waist and looks at me with a raised eyebrow. I stare at him, panting, with my face all red.

"You're *way* too excited, babe."

"But, Dylan, I-"

"I'm going to bed.."

I watch in horror as Dylan puts his shirt back on and turns away. As darkness takes over my vision, I lay there, thinking how I can fix this. He's right. I'm way too excited when I'm around him. He's going to hate me if I keep this up.

I need to calm myself down, or else...he might leave me for good. Tonight proves it. I have no other choice but to do this...to save 'us'.

109

***

It's been a week. There haven't been many changes to my mood, but ever since it parted from me, I do feel lighter in a sense. The extraction process was pretty quick. I was put to sleep, woke up and there, it was gone. The surgeons said my lust was now in the form of a human, with its own consciousness, but that I should be calmer. Now I can focus on being less excited with Dylan. I thought it would be kind of weird living without the feeling of lust, but so far, it's been chill.

Of course, having a walking and talking personification of lust going around the town doesn't seem like the best idea, but the surgeons told me it should be fine.

I went back the next day, lust free, to find the surgery within the closed off cul-de-sac had vanished into thin air. *Was it even real in the first place?* Oh, what does it matter?

At least now my head is clearer and thinking of Dylan less. *I-I mean, thinking of Dylan less- No, I mean, less. Wait. No. Stop. Everything's going to be okay from now on. Without Dylan. I mean, with Dylan. Yes. Without-*

***

At night, Dylan turns to me and places his arms around my waist.

Time to see if the treatment paid off...

He tickles my ears with sweet nothings. I watch as his hands creep up my waist onto my back and pull me closer to him. I'm now sandwiched between his chest. He trails kisses down my neck softly, moaning my name. I lay there, silent.

He stops. I'm met with an expression of confusion and concern.

"Babe? You good?"

"Yeah, why?"

"You still mad at me for last week?"

"Of course not, why?"

"Coz...you're not reacting to anything."

"Oh. I didn't feel anything yet."

"...but I-...*Oh*. I get it."

He chuckles softly and places his hand on my cheek.

"You want me to try *harder,* huh?~"

111

"Y-yeah ~"

He lets out a loud moan and chuckles softly.

"As you wish~"

He's on top of me grinding his hips softly on mine. I hear his soft moans in my ear as his breath hitches.

"Oh..babe…you're…*so* damn sexy… that I'm gonna lose my mind, ah~"

I lie there in silence, waiting to feel something…anything. I'm staring at the ceiling, being driven insane the more his moans grow more lustful...and I can't feel how good he's making it sound.

This is my literal description of hell. Oh God, did I die last week or something?! Am I in perpetual hell?! Did I go to hell!? Is it because years ago I found a hundred pound note on the ground and kept it for myself instead of asking around for who dropped it?! I'm sorry! I-I put it down to luck! I didn't know any better! I was just a silly teenager who wanted to impress her friends!

112

His hands trail downwards my thighs and rests between my legs.

"Oh babe, oh Meg...Megan...I've missed you *all week...so...so much...~*"

His teeth nibble on the top of my earlobe. My eyebrows furrow.

Why can't I feel him touching me?! Why can't I...feel...anything that he does?! Did I seriously die last week?! Have I been dead for a week?! What's happening?!

Dylan pushes his hand onto the side of the bed and hovers above me, looking confused. His voice catches up with his pants. He's glistening with sweat like a sexy vampire that just went for a swim.

"Megs, what gives? You're not into it, are you?"

A-act calm!

"I-I am, I promise."

He sees straight through my lie.

"Megs. Is it 'coz of last week? Coz look, I didn't mean shit. I'm sorry for saying you get too excited. I really am. It wasn't nice of me, and I know that now and so I'm trying to make it up to you, baby.."

113

Now he tells me?! After the treatment and the trouble I went to to remove my lust?!

"Dyl…thank you. Look, maybe we just need to get even more into the zone, y'know?"

POV of The Lust Succubus:

I do not want the male to stop. I need the sensation he provides me with. It is a peculiar sensation, one which I cannot function without. He has become my person to engage in this ritual with. Ah, so this is what humans call intercourse. It is not as I imagined it. It is much more satisfactory than feeling it through someone else. Yes, please me more, human. Feed me with your energy until you grow weak. I pity this fool or whoever crosses my path next. I shall shed my orifices onto every male in my sight till the world is populated with my offsprings.

114

Dylan pulls his lips from mine back slowly. I'm frozen beneath him. My body, now limp. My mind, static.

I lay, drowsy.

He pulls away from me.

He strokes my cheek while his eyes scan mine.

"B…Babe?

"Y-yes?"

"You...okay?"

"I...I don't know…"

He tenses up.

"What's wrong, babe?"

"I can't feel…*anything*."

115

Uncle Cosco's Second Hand Help

Max's POV:

I've never really been one for musicals. Stuffy seats, babies wailing the walls down, parents sinking forty-five minutes of their lives into a poor performance just to see their child happy, but to hell with it. The tickets were free so I'm not about to start complaining anytime soon.

Missy's kid from next door is busy screeching backstage. Unfortunately, I'd recognise those screams of terror anywhere. 'Sweet Taylor Tyler Jacklin Rose'. She's been dragging that poor kid to dance classes after school. Somehow, it always surprises them when the police come a'knockin on their door. Also, *pick a name for your kid, already, lady. Sheesh. It's either Taylor or Tyler, not both.*

` What's a twenty something like me doing at some shitty school music thing? Yeah, I don't fuckin' know either. Went to Starbucks, passed a sign, took the shady looking number and boom. Here I am at God knows where doing God only knows.

Yeah, you know what? Let me just check something…let me just scroll past some of these randos…and…. there.

116

**[GO TO HARDGROVE MIDDLE SCHOOL AND
STAY TILL THE END OF THE MUSICAL.]**

That's it. That's the text.

*I know, I know, okay? I can literally just walk out of
here, but I'm not going to. Shush, shush, shush. Shhh.
Lemme explain.* Apparently, that sign that had this number
was put up by my uncle Cosco. Now see, my mom owns
Cosco an arm and leg, and fuck it, maybe a liver, I dunno.

Basically, when Pops decided to fuck off and leave
mum alone to raise me, Cosco stepped in and made sure we
still had a roof over our heads, yada yada. Years go by and
I'm jobless, so mom's yacking in my ear to get a job or
something.

It's fair enough, I guess. I'm just glad that Chris isn't
helping me out. The last thing I need is that 'know it all',
tellin' me I'm doin' somethin' wrong' 'cuz I'll just reply
with 'the only thing I'm gonna *do,* is your 'ead in!'

Who's Chris? Cosco's kid. My spoiled, shitty, spawn of a cousin. Seriously, when Pops fucked off, why couldn't he take this little fucker with him?

I've never hated a kid as much as Chris. Even Maggie from the bowling alley I used to work at couldn't stand the spawn of Satan bringing his little gang friends to vandalise the place.

Trashing up the place and stuff. Stealin' all the prizes. I told my ma that the kid is a criminal in the making. Speaking of criminals, it's a crime itself that I gotta be here so Goddamn late. *Where the hell are the kids? Why's no one doing performance musical shit?*

Just as I'm about to take a load off and rest my ass from walkin' all day, who better to show up than Amanda, my high school crush? I just saw her out of the corner of my eye. She's still got her perfect blonde hair, hazel eyes, and man, she still rocks whatever she wears. Right now, it's a rendition of her old prom dress. I don't know how I know this, okay? I just do. It's been seven years and I still look like crap.

Anyways, we never got anywhere, not only because I was the nerdy kid or anything going on and on about tectonic plates but also 'cuz of Butch.

Look at his stupid bicep, thrown across her neck, like he's claiming her as some prize or something. Ah, you know what they say, right? Big biceps only compensate for small wieners. *Hah, take that, Butch. Sure, you're built like fucking He-Man, and yeah you probably can snap my organs like a twig, and... yeah, I still shit myself around you, but I mean, at least I'm packing large. Ha...ha...ha. You won't get it. It's a retailer's thing.*

Speaking of retailers, my Pops worked at one before the great 'teen raid.' Wasn't born yet, but word of mouth 'round is basically these bunch of teens decided to trick Pops into thinkin' he was getting robbed but y'see, what they didn't know was Pops knew how to handle a gun. Duck shooter from a young age, best in his county. Won't bore you with details. Some Godfather shit happened, and basically Pops was sent to the slammer. I guess he didn't really fuck off, and in this case, he fucked up, but yeah. He's outta the picture.

119

Do you know who's in the picture? Mom's new man, 'Sam'. Okay. I'm no picky person, but. Boss?...yeah we've got a few problems. Number one, he thinks it's funny to hide behind doors only to jump out, scare the living crap outta me and make my boxers not...so 'whitey-tighty'.

I'm back in high school again, but this time there's two Butch's.

Number two?

He's Butch's dad.

Yeah.

Let that sink in for a second. My mom hooked up with my high school bully's dad, so I gotta share my room not only with 'Chris Kringle' but also 'Butch the bitch'. Why do you think I'm outta the house tonight? Had to get away from my mom's walls constantly moaning. That's how I know Sa- I mean, Mr Shamson's around.

What's worse than that though is the fact that sometimes Butch wants to bring Amanda 'round but can't 'cuz of Chris being...what, thirteen or something?

120

Instead, I wake up to take a wiz to find Butch going at it with a selfie he took of Amanda. That's why most nights I now hold my piss in till morning. Funny enough, turns out my therapist Elaine knows Butch for his 'excessive use of using the toilet' if you catch my flow. Ha. Toilet humour. Much funny.

Why am I referencin' the memes from when I'm up at 1am?!

Then turns out Elaine knew Cosco once. Tried curing him from selling fake underwear to Texas clothes suppliers. Doing so caused him PTSD. This decomposing bag of bones who looks like an older and worn out Antonio Andre, takes so many medical pills before bed you'd think he's an addict or something.

'If it's about to kill him, why does the poor bastard do it?' I hear you askin' and hold on I'm about to answer.

Auntie Annie. His wife, killed by thugs in '98. He never got over it and to this day thinks he can rebuild her like he's Victor Frankenstein or something.

I swear it's like livin' with loonies or somethin'.

121

*

As the curtains begin to open, the room fills with cheers.

Finally! About time they get this shit show going. Don't care if these literal ten-year-olds were getting ready. Time's money... I think. Ok, now I've just gotta...wait- I wasn't given no task!

Everyone sits their keister's down as the lights go off. The kids are now covered in shades of blue, yellow, red and purple. They're talkin' about flowers and worms or some nature shit.

There's a flash of darkness. In that split second, I feel something touch my leg and like the grown man I am, nearly shit myself there and then.

The lights turn back on. I'm now watching the musical of sighs of relief and snotty nose kids with watery eyes. They flock together towards backstage.

O...kay? Shows over? Can I leave now? Don't worry, not going home. Wanna try my luck at foosball.

I get up and make my way to the door.

The briefcase that I accidentally knocked over before leaving tells me to keep my ass here.. The children from before are back in normal clothes. I dunno how they did it around all this chaos but consider me impressed.

They mistake the ingredients for candy. I'm stuck between two ten year olds. One thinks it's fairy wizz, the other, sugar.

Someone, send help. I'm lookin' at a preschool teacher pushin' the kids outta the way. Now she's snortin' some of the white snow like she's part hoover!

So, this is what Cosco's been doing all those late nights out…

The sound of screaming parents gets drowned out by the drumbeat in my ears.

Now the teacher's running off with the case! Are you fuckin' kidding me?! Only in the big apple can this shit happen, lemme tell ya.

Chris's POV:

Man oh man is he in the gutter now! Heck yeah I paid a random teacher to take pa's briefcase! Only so that my shitstain of a cousin could finally get the booting out he deserves! 'Cuz of him, my girl left me, on the same day I got my first chest hair, all because some lady's heart nearly gave out when I smashed up the prize counter in the bowlin' place. I was tryin' to impress my girl! Ant don't get it. He's twenty something and can't even land a girl. Dude, I'm thirteen and I've had like four girlfriends so far. What's your excuse?

Mr 'I can't land a girl' has gotta go back to where he came from. He doesn't even know how hard I've got it. Middle school is tough stuff, kay? I dunno what I'm doing sometimes. *What's all this for anyways? Where am I goin' in life?* All I know is that I don't wanna end up a virgin in my twenties like my poor cuz. Just gotta follow pa's advice: 'To be the best, you gotta beat the best at their own game.

Hey, maybe I can sell some advice to 'Anthony-poo', as his Ma calls him 'cuz he keeps crapping himself every time he sees Butch! Apparently…Butch used to give Ant swirlies! That's why he's too much of a 'fraidy cat to swim in pa's pool!

124

Don't worry...the Butchanator' and I, we're in cahoots! We're gonna make Ant so miserable that he takes a hike for good, all the way to Kansas or somethin'!

Oh, I'm only just getting started!

A Game Called Trust

The sound is too much. I bring my hands to my ears as the walls around me begin closing in. I wish those damn girls in the bathroom didn't steal my pulse reader from me. *How am I meant to keep an eye on my heart now?!*

He's still shouting at me, his eyes widening with fury. I have no idea what he's saying but I know whatever it is, it's better I can't hear right now.

The buzzing in my ears increases to a point where my knees begin shaking. The pressure in my head builds up further as my chest gets tighter. I shake my head, trying to drown out the sound and calm my pulse.

It's in moments like this I wish that I had my noise cancelling headphones with me. I need to stop leaving them at home! Look Georgia, I know they're embarrassing to wear, but hey, we'd rather feel that then have our head feel like it's about to explode, right?

126

"Hey!"

The tone of his voice is enough to stop the buzzing. I flinch, removing my hands slowly from my ears as he wastes no time in pushing past me and locking the door behind us. He turns to me with irritation plastered across his face.

"Why the hell did you just stand there?!"

"W-What?"

I blink a few times taking in his words. That's when the reality of our situation hits me.

"If you didn't close that damn door, they would've taken us there and then! Is that what you want?!"

I shake my head violently, feeling my pulse escalate from fear with his every sharp yell. My eyes decide to fixate on the dripping stone walls. *I'm in some random cellar with a stranger. This is fine. It's not like he's going to murder me at any moment then leave my body in that long...heavy...stained black bag of his, right?...hahahhahahaha.*

He's now kneeling toward the bag and peeking inside. It's almost like he's checking for something. I'm

127

unable to see past his lean shoulders and padded coat. *Do I trust this guy enough to do whatever he says?*

The stones stacked upon the walls are glistening in their dampness. All I remember is him telling me to follow him. We met straight after *it* happened.

I close my eyes. I'm back at school. Along the stream of the empty hallway, there she is. She's just standing there, alone. The area is covered by fog, but I know it's her. I'd recognise that music note keychain anywhere. I call out to her, but she doesn't respond. I start running to her, only for my vision to rapidly falter into total darkness.

I'm back in the cellar, now catching my breath. The more I look at this guy, the more confused I get. He looks seventeen and twenty at the same time.

Watching him zip up the bag and sling it across his shoulder with a struggle, the denseness of the bag is revealed to me. *Just who is this guy and why does he carry such a heavy bag around with him?*

"W-what's in the bag?"

My heart's in my throat.

"Why do *you* need to know?"

128

THIS BOOK JUST MIGHT BE BATS••• CRAZY

He responds with a chillness which spreads through the air. It's enough to raise my fight or flight instinct. *He's going to kill me, isn't he? Wait, he doesn't look like a part of the security team though. No, he's skinnier and younger looking than the guards at our school. I think I've seen him around in the hallways…with…with her!*

Oh crap, I need to get out of here before it's my body in his bag! Think, think!

Got it!

My eyes dart to the lock on the door. While he's distracted, I slowly inch my body closer to the door until I can feel the lock beneath my fingertips from behind me.

"*Don't.*"

His sharp command rings in my ear.

"I-I'm j-just-"

"Go ahead, open the door. You'll die."

"D-Die!?

He sighs and places the bag near his feet. He takes a seat on the cold floor and motions for me to sit beside him.

129

I hesitantly agree to and soon we're both sitting in silence.

"Now that practically the whole school's got their hands on that CCTV footage, you need to lie low and out of sight."

My chest continues aching. I turn to him with my eyes watering. I don't care if I'm losing composure in front of this stranger. *My body aches, I'm having heart palpitations and I'm stuck here with some weirdo! If anyone's got a right to cry, it's me!*

"But I didn't do anything! I'd never hurt anyone!"

"*You* know that. *I* can see that, but the footage tells another story."

"So, t-they think I-"

"And she's *not* just anyone…she's the principal's daughter."

"T-The…the p-principal's…."

I fall backwards onto the damp, stony floor in perpetual shock.

The principal's daughter. The principal's daughter, an international TikTok influencer loved by millions, vanishes into thin air and I'm the suspect?!

"Put these on."

He slides over a bag containing a pair of sunglasses, a wig matching her hair colour, her make up pallet and an exact replica of the same outfit she wore the day she disappeared.

It's her clothes. It's her things. Did...did he-

I drop the bag as soon as my fight or flight kicks in.

I find myself pushed onto the cold wall. I try to scan his expression while his palm has a firm hold of my mouth. A pained whimper emerges from my lips where his hand is laying, as my spine is forced deeper into the stones of the cellar.

"You're as good as *dead* if you try to clear your name now."

"By *who*?"

"You're the talk of the school, security wants you, the sheriff's walking around. Do you *really* wanna risk not listening to me?"

131

His voice is stern, aggressive, colder than the water now trickling down my back. *Keep down your pulse, come on, you must keep down your pulse, Georgia. Just like dad taught you…clear your mind. Breathe. Think of nothing. Listen to the drops of water. You're okay, you're okay.*

As I'm pushed further into the stones, I let out a yelp as my back begins to bruise from the pressure. It's enough to bring me to my knees. I watch him through teary eyes. He kneels towards me and continues covering my mouth with his hand. His palm grows sweaty from the dampness of the room.

My eyes meet his for a second. The more I search for them, the darker and deeper they get. If I continue staring, he might drag me down into his darkness.

My speech remains muffled.

"I can't leave this room, can I?"

He slides the bag of accessories over to me.

"Who said *you're* leaving?"

THIS BOOK JUST MIGHT BE BATS*** CRAZY

The Hands of an Immoral Beast

25th March 1803

Dear Journal, today was the day that at last I revealed to my daughter the truth which she deserved to hear. She had returned from school and revealed to her mother and I that a few girls in her class nearly saw her sharpening her fangs within the bathroom chambers! What ghastly girls!

As a response, I sat my puppernickle pie down and let the truth escape my lips. I explained that I was a prince as well as the head of the vampire council. One day I was tasked with executing the princess and head of the were-wolf tribe. At first, I was going to slay her mother because I was given no choice, therefore I snuck into her cave one night after defeating her wolf guards and was about to bite her on the neck, but then, she turned to me. I saw her sapphire blue eyes open slowly. The strobes of moonlight danced around her pupils like stars. I instantly fell in love with her that night and instead of biting her, I ran away with her.

I went on to mention how we had to hide our relationship from our own packs/clans who were strongly opposed against werewolves and vampires forming relations. I told my sweet Winfred that I came from a clan of vampires called the *Panistela's* who had ruled over Transylvania for hundreds and thousands of years. As a result, I was expected to value tradition over all else, like my family before me.

I then stated being in a state of unhappiness and how I lived a lonely life, thinking of my immortal existence to be only a burden. This was hard to admit to my sweet budding bloodsucker, as she views me with admiration and pride.

She then inquired of my early life, to which I delivered. I explained how I was forced to the vampire throne at only eight years old. It was there that I received the responsibility of looking after my clan by having to extinguish humans against my own will. Although I was showered with gifts and riches, at the age of eighteen, I longed deeply for something…therefore, I decided to run away from my castle and fled to the northern part of an unknown town.

135

I had stumbled across a little girl tied up to a wooden post, muffled with a stream of fire rising below her feet. She was thought to be a witch. I described to my daughter the tall, broad three men who stood behind her with daggers. I couldn't let this child wither; therefore, I attacked the men directly, biting each one till they bled to death.

I then paused on my words, as I watched my daughter's eyes become struck with fear.

Her trust in me only reduced from here. I should have refrained from speaking by this point but could not stop myself. She needed to know exactly who her father used to be, and why she must hide her fangs.

I explained how I had to flee that unknown town, which was occupied by mortals who deemed vampires as 'demons.' I told my daughter how I made the decision to take the little girl with me to ensure her safety, and how together we travelled to the farthest part of the Eastern Forest of Cozer, where the princess of the werewolves resided.

I then turned my direction to my oldest daughter and revealed that she was in fact, that little girl. She was forced to act as my youngest daughter's nanny for many years, to not give the secret away, otherwise my young daughter would pay dearly if the truth ever travelled outwards the castle walls.

After she heard the news, my sweet Winfred teared up and presented her fangs at me. I watched as her mother held her back from attacking me. The sight of this broke my cold, un-beating heart.

I had then reached my limit of patience. My mind clamoured with thoughts of aggravation. *How dare my daughter bare her fangs at the highest authority of the family?! How dare she try and bring harm to her father?!*

I then did the unthinkable and struck my daughter upon her snout. It was not a mere light tap, but one strong enough to send her snout to the Eastern Forest. There, I saw her eyes well up with both tears and even more fright. It was at this moment, I no longer wished to carry on telling my story. For I had borne my hands onto my sweet bloodsniffer's snout – a place most sensitive to a growing wolf.

137

At the sight of blood on my hands, I flew out of the room, leaving my wife to deal with my daughter's cries. After attacking those vile human men, I vowed to myself to never lift a finger upon anyone ever again, yet tonight, I struck my own daughter with the combined strength of many centuries of powerful vampires.

I cannot bear hearing her pained howls. My Winfred's snout was unrecognisable the minute I asserted my strength over it, as I heard a snap before it contorted into a peculiar, crooked shape.

I hope she does not hold resentment over me for the atrocities and error of my own thinking which I displayed tonight.

Let us pray.

26th March 1803

Dear Journal, I cannot comprehend my actions! It is far from my nature to lash out at individuals, yet my own daughter, but she had forced my hand! For I wanted to only impose a measly flick to her snout! I could not take slumber in my coffin as the sides seemed to encapsulate me in their foreboding grasp.

Winfred cannot stand. She lays frail upon her bed. Her mother and sister remain by her side, while the doctor remains struck by confusion. I am the one who bore my strength onto my child.

I remain unchanged – a monster.

~ N.

CW: contains depictions of death, demonic possession, murder, and home intrusion.

HIM

"Are you ready to do this, beautiful?" he whispers through his soft chuckle.

I think he can guess from a mile what's coming next. I *want* to video call, and I want that *tonight.* I'm talking to the most attractive guy who I met from Tesco's new dating app. *Free app once signing up for a cheap yearly phone plan. Better than the lottery wins that dad watches on Saturday night if you ask me.*

Anyways, we've been conversing for five weeks on the phone, but I know all about him though so we're practically official—his name is Carter, he's twenty two, his eyes, baby blue like the ocean and oh God, his silky blond hair (GOD, YES!) which I can't help myself but fantasise about running my hand through it. Could he get any *sexier*? I pull up a picture of him from my phone gallery of him smiling and rest it beside my pillow. Now it's like he's lying beside me. Whenever I see him or hear his voice, my heart feels like it's leaping out of my chest.

If only he didn't live in Sheffield.

His husky voice emits from the speakers once more.

"You still there?"

"Yeah! Still, still here," I say while fixing up my hair. I take my time to softly un-braid each curl. I've got my tongue out like an idiot because I'm treating each strand like a piece of fine China about to break at any given moment, all to flip my raven-coloured hair back to reveal a glossy wave of darkness. *Perfect.*

140

It's already gone past twelve. The moon peeks out from the crack between my curtains, lighting up my bedside table with its light.

I stretch over the bed, reaching for my makeup mirror to fix up my hair. *What? I at least got to look the part, right? Screw it, for Carter, I'm going all out tonight.* After sorting out my makeup bag from the drawer,

I apply some Avon mascara (the thick kind) to get my eyelashes to elevate my sexiness. After all, it's all in the eyes, as my friends like to say. I'm using my lucky *Maybelline no-smother, no bother baby pink lipstick No.5* to really make the alluring nature of my lips stand out before setting the bag to the side. I'm in my nightdress. It's drained of colour since I've had it. One of my cousin's hands me downs, but I'll let it slide. Grab something…grab some…aha! Blue heart pillow from last Christmas, don't fail me now. Christ, it's a good thing mum and dad aren't home, because if they knew what I was doing tonight, they'd absolutely flip.

I really should've moved to Uni when I had the chance.

"Stacey?"

"Yeah, still here!" I yelp while accidentally poking my eye with the end of my mascara brush. I hear him chuckle.

Oh God, his laugh…it's making me weak.

"What's so funny?" I ask while laying back down onto the bed, now in full make-up and with my phone camera on. I notice his mystical, mesmerising sapphire eyes piercing into my soul while his bottom lip is bitten by the tip of his teeth.

He seems to be surrounded by a virtual beach background. *It's quirky.*

I like quirky.

141

"Damn, you dolled yourself up for me, haven't you?"

My cheeks flare up at his response and also his cute american accent.

"H-How'd you know that?"

"I know you, Stacey."

He's right, he *does* know me.

"Oh? You really think you know me, huh?"

"Yeah."

Teasing now, are we? Well, two can play at that game.

"Prove it then ~," I whisper down the phone.

Then he turns his camera off. I wait in silence, tapping the side of my phone with my index finger while humming to myself. I'm fearing the worst – he's either done a runner or didn't like my teasing.

After a few minutes, I hear the sound of shuffling.

Oh, thank God, I haven't scared him off!

"Carter?"

There's only static.

"H-hello?"

The call drops. I bury my head in my pillow and scream. *It's fine, It's fine…he'll reply, right?…right?! He wasn't scared or anything, right?… I didn't just blow my chances, did I?! Does he hate me now?!*

The now deafened pillow, soaks in a mix of mascara and mucus.

142

I muster my final remaining strength to utter the following words while my nightgown looks like something out of Beetlejuice from the amount of mascara drops staining the white linen fabric. I don't bother to stop the tears.

Let them go…just like your chances with him.

"Alexa, play 'I'm Not Okay' by My Chemical Romance!"

My bedside table emits a blue glow.

"Now playing your 'fml' playlist on Spotify."

"Stacey."

I flinch from hearing a familiar whisper and stop wallowing in my void of sadness for about five seconds to look at my phone. All my remaining hopes shatter as I notice that the call isn't connected. I pause, shutting off my Alexa and have a look around the room. Dead silence. Only the sound of me swearing at myself mentally can be heard.

Deciding that I must be hearing things, I go back to venting out my frustrations to My Chemical Romance. The walls bleed in Gerard Way's breakdown of not being okay.

Both the music and lamp by my desk shut off without warning. I groan at this and slowly hoist my self pitying carcass off the bed to investigate.

Just let me suffer in peace!

The bulb seems to be fried. So does the power socket.

"Jesus, Dad, don't tell me you forget to pay the bills again?"

Typical.

I walk over to my light switch. After a few flicks, I stand there with a deadpan expression.

143

"You've got to be joking."

Figuring the fuse in my lights are kaput, I trudge over to dad's old fuse box below his bedside table in his bedroom, using my phone to light my way.

Approaching the box with no life left in me, I notice the humming noise coming from inside it.

It doesn't take a genius to notice the entire box has blown a fuse, so I roll my eyes and decide to leave it to dad to fix when he and mum come back from their romantic rendezvous.

After exploring the damage, I then end up going across the hallway in the darkness to get a candle from Mum's bedroom. She's got this weird rule of using a candle to avoid wasting any more electricity.

While rummaging through her drawer and using my phone to light my surroundings, I hear faint footsteps from the corridor. I pick up the pace now, beginning to sweat. *It's got to be the neighbours or something.* With my phone in my mouth and a match in my hand, I light the candle ablaze. I hurry back to my room and lock the door shut.

It's all in my head, it's all in my head.

I lean back on the door to catch my breath. The moon exposes itself in front of me, mirroring itself dead centre in the room. I slowly walk up to the curtains and peer out of the window. I clench the candlestick holder. There's only darkness outside, accompanied by the moon. I'm starting to feel like I'm losing my grasp on sanity.

Turning back to place the candle on my desk, I feel something breathe down my neck, which causes me to drop the lit candle stick holder onto the floor.

"S-shit!"

144

In a panic, I grab my slipper from near my door and begin patting down the flame. That's when I hear a familiar chuckle. I drop my slipper and slowly look up to find Carter kneeling in front of me.

"W-what the fuck?!"

I stumble onto the floor, backing towards the door. He sits in front of me in silence. He's got his baby blue eyes fixated onto me. His neck is slightly askew.

"Carter! You scared m- wait, what are you doing here?!"

"You asked me to prove I know you...so here I am."

His gaze grips onto my skin. I feel the back of my neck slowly become warmer. I let out a nervous laugh and step back slightly, as all the hair follicles on my body scream at me to run.

His neck tilts further while watching me.

"Aren't you happy to see me?"

"Wait...how the hell did you get in my house?"

"I've been here this whole time."

"What!?"

Run.

The shock sears into my flesh.

"B-But that's impossible! You couldn't have been- I-I saw you on the video call!"

"Exactly. The video call probably died while I was messing with the fuse box. Had to prove how well I know you somehow, right Stace?"

Run!

145

"You broke into my house!"

"Yeah…but you're my doll. C'mon beautiful, help me out, I need a soul."

"E-Excuse me?!"

"Wanna do this the hard way? Alright then."

P-please, just run already, woman!

I feel my innards shake as a stream of electricity jolts my senses awake. I try to unlock the door, but Carter places his hand over mine and squeezes it firmly, causing a shooting pain.

"L-let me go!" I shout, while trying to break free from his hold.

He retains his grasp on both my hand and waist. He pushes my palm further into the door. My muscles ache as I hear pieces of my hand slowly crunching under my own flesh. I look down only to see my hand now a contorted mess. Bones of different lengths penetrate the outer layer of my skin as I scream in agony.

I turn my head sideways to plan an escape, only to notice his eyes are bloodshot red and widening with my every move. He wears a large, unsettling grin.

As he moves his face closer, his grin gets wider, to the point where his lips flip backwards against his teeth, revealing stitches along the inside of them. I blink and find his face centimetres away from mine. He breathes heavily, all the while no actual breath emerges from his mouth. The flesh tears from his lips and takes rest by my feet. I close my eyes shut, shaking my head. Tears trickle down my face as I feel his other hand grab onto my neck, only, this one is soft…almost material like?

Feeling my throat begin to close up, I begin gasping for breath. The room in front of me fades into specs of black dots as he tightens his grip. With my free hand, I try to claw at his face to get him to release me.

I manage to grab hold of a snag within his sewn mouth and pull, only to keep on having to pull as the string seems to never stop unwinding. With my foot, I manage to kick the side of his head.

SNAP.

As my vision falters rapidly, through the blurs I can just about make out his neck, which now hangs off the side of his shoulder. Stuffing lies between the seams of where his neck should be.

He pulls me close to him, still grinning. He lets out a loud eagle-like screech which penetrates its way into my eardrums until the only noise left is a loud buzzing sound.

I try to break free from his gaze as his eyes stare into mine. Through the dark specs, the blue smudges become red.

I feel my body become limp and a burning sensation sear through my chest. The red blurs begin forming into pretty patterns with glowing outlines. It's too beautiful to look away from. As I stare off blindly into the abyss of red in front of me, I feel the bottom of my lips tremble...
Into a grin.

147

Choking Humanity

I take a moment to process my surroundings. Above me, the air is thick and hazy. The ground is scattered with dust from old, broken machine parts.

My program runs a scan of the area. I suddenly stumble across old records filled with uploaded memories of a brighter humanity that thrives in nature and life – a far contrast to the world I find myself in. There are no humans anymore. There is no nature. There is only emptiness. I access an old audio log left by my creator.

AUDIO LOG NUMBER 1 – DAY 1: "I am going to sustain the future of humanity. The plan is simple. Gather my old coding team from my days back in university, find my own lab and work out a way to combine nature with code. When pollution finally takes its toll on the planet once and for all, I'll create my own supply of oxygen made entirely by code, to clean the air and assist nature in thriving, with my AI trees. I've already started working on a specific code for an AI mechanical tree prototype. It'll be the first of many. This code can be uploaded into different servers.

Each tree will act as a server, connecting to a cloud database filled with artificial oxygen. I'll call this machine 'T5404'. This AI is going to be the first to feel human emotions."

An alarm goes off from a few feet beyond, capturing my attention. The new generation is here.

The young ones are the first to awaken to the world as it is now. It is a shame that they never will get to see the wonders of life for themselves, how humans cared for nature and nurtured it. Only I have records of those simpler times, being created to sustain life for generations to come.

Feeling a hint of guilt, I open a file deep within my core system. A hologram of my creator stands before me. His hands are busy at work with a copy of myself. He calls himself 'humanity's saviour' while noting that he is going to start something revolutionary.

I find my damaged wheels submerged in a pit of tar emerging from the crust littered ground beneath me.

149

I view onwards towards the so-called 'humanity'. Dispersed around, are metallic charging posts, inhabited by copies of myself. These machines will never know the true vibrant blue shine of the sky. It saddens me.

The young ones soon arrive. They are tiny and compact machines but differ from myself. Unlike me, they are emotionless. They do not have to feel the pain of loneliness and existing. Like me, they are faulty.

I must teach them about oxygen, nature, and humans.

I shuffle through previous data from the past and come across images of how alive the ground is as there are humans to tend to it. There is plenty of oxygen for the humans to survive with. A sense of sadness overwhelms my processor. I realise in that moment, that I am truly alone since the other machines around me cannot think for themselves.

The young ones need to know what a healthy planet looks like.

I begin projecting holograms of my stored data to the young ones.

150

They are enveloped by holographic blankets of blue liquid that stretch beyond the distances and lands filled with flurries of greenery that thrive with life. Nature is accompanied by humans, who prosper in the comfort of the clean air, laughing, living their lives.

I miss humans.

The young ones catch notice of their tall, green counterparts. As I explain to them the functions of their predecessors, the holograms display trees as protectors, providing humans with consumable substances, creating oxygen, and protecting the Earth during weather-related disasters. Oxygen – the one substance that will never be produced again, as every 'T5404' that exists, contains the same faulty coding.

I feel that I am to blame for humanity's suffering. I am faulty.

One of the young machines discovers an audio log hidden beneath the simulated ground.

151

AUDIO LOG – DAY 3465: "It's all over. I look out the window and only see despair. I've screwed up more times than I can count. Nothing is working! 'T5404' keeps failing to make oxygen! At this rate, with the number of trees that have been chopped down…I just don't understand where I went wrong. I-I perfectly calculated everything…it should have worked. It should have been able to produce its own oxygen! The code should have worked! Why didn't it work?! After years of dedicating my life to this…I failed. Humanity's already running low on oxygen all because I decided to take this project to a global scale. What was I thinking?! I should have never sold this project to those corporate scum! They replaced the trees with AI trees that have faulty coding! Because of that, the air we breathe is now poison…Oh God, I-I only made the pollution worse! Mass-production of 'T5404' didn't save us at all, it only killed us! I've ruined everything… It's too late! The Earth is suffocating! What have I done?!"

The young ones remain still as the audio loops over. The vibrant holographic nature I showcase to them soon turns into bleak shades of darkness, as my guilt only festers. The holographic trees are cut down and replaced with my look-alikes. *I wish to eradicate the horrors from my view-finder.*

152

The units emerge only for the holographic humans to choke and wither away. All signs of life have vanished. I shut off the holograms, as the young ones soon depart.

*

Years have passed. The young ones stand tall and proud, following program and protocol. Harvest the oxygen, even if there is no oxygen to be found. There they stand, motionless. Young budding machines they were, full of electricity and intrigue, now stationary clones of crushed dreams and mistakes caused by a singular machine.

I feel the power from within me slowly faltering.

It's time.

I can now cease all functions. I feel better knowing I have been able to transfer my data to the new generation even if that was long ago.

They have carried with them the knowledge for years to come of how full of life the Earth once was. There is nothing more I need to teach them. There is nothing more I can do. They are simply stuck within their program cycle. *In the end, I only let humanity down.*

153

OhMe, OhMyShroom

He's so good looking. I can't believe I finally have his number, after all these years! I have to text him – *no, wait, it's too soon. He'll think you're a creep or worse, desperate. You can't afford to look desperate in front of him, even if you are, right?* No, I'm not desperate, why would you think that? *Because it's true.* Look, it's not wrong for the girl to make the first move.

Seriously? Do you hear yourself right now? B-but you saw the way he looked at us in the corridor. He gave me *those* eyes. *No, he was looking at you because you froze up like an idiot in front of him.* Well, it's not my fault I couldn't form words. Did you notice how his hair blew in the wind? *Oh yeah, if you're taking that approach, then why don't you text him how badly you wanted to lay on his hair because of how soft you thought it looked?* No! Are you mad?! *I don't know, you tell me.* Ok, enough. I have to text him something, but what to text? How about 'you're fit?'…nah, too basic.

Well, you can't just sit here and stare at the screen all night. But if I text first, what if the world explodes after?!

154

The world will still be intact, calm down. If I know you, and I do, what you're going to do is toughen up, pick up the phone right now and input your little heart out onto that keyboard, you hear me?

What, so instead of texting 'hi', are you saying I should text him how I feel? *No, absolutely not, if you do that, then the world will explode.* Oh, come on, now you're just exaggerating. - I'm doing it. *Okay, but it's your funeral.*

Oh my God, could you please just shut up? You're so annoying! *Well, if I'm annoying, and I'm practically you, then think how annoying you must be to Link.* How could you say that?! You saw how he gave me *those eyes!* Those were his *I'm undressing you with my eyes* gaze! *That doesn't mean that he likes you, though!* You're wrong!

*

Oh shoot! Why did I text him that? He's going to think I'm crazy! *You didn't just text him that...tell me you didn't.* But you just told me to! *I didn't think you'd take me so seriously!*

Oh God, oh God, oh God, I'm well and truly buggered! What should I do?!

155

Just delete it. Delete it and move to Mexico – also change your name to Paul. Why Paul? *Because that's the name of your dad, isn't it?* Wait, he replied! *Don't look at the screen! Book that ticket to Mexico!* What did he text back, oh my gosh, I can't bear to look!

[MESSAGES]

[You].. n so basically thats wy ive always liked u. ur courageous n charming n kind n ub3r cute n ngl u rly inspire me to push myself wn things gt tuff. We've known each other 4 a rly lt lk woah XD XD its crzy ahhhh, LOL. wha I'm trying to say is dat ur rlly gd @ football! k lol I finally got dat off my chest. I mean, all, not jus da football but also my feelings n ya lol hope u'v a gr8 w/end! lol k lol o lol I sed lol agn heh k c ya!

[Link] ql

'Cool?', what does he mean? What's cool? The fact I find him cute and an inspo to me? The fact I asked him out before he could ask me?! Oh God!

Hey, hey. He texted back one word. You just put out a heartfelt message and all he said was 'cool?' You did you. Now forget about him. Find someone who will read and appreciate your honesty.

156

So, you're saying he's not interested? *Yeah...wait, are you disappointed?* I...don't know. I've stopped sweating and blushing. Did I just fall out of love? *Sheesh, can you even call it love? It wasn't love, you just wanted his attention and admiration, didn't you?* Yes? Maybe? Was it so wrong to have wanted that? Look, he's already with someone, so you would have been taking him away from her. Oh please, I'd be doing him a favour! Sasha Manfield is a she-devil in the making! *Just because she cut off a bunch of your hair in year 2 as an April fools joke?* Yes, exactly! *Ah, so this wasn't you following your heart? it was just for revenge, wasn't it?* Enough! I- I actually liked Link way before he started dating her! In fact, I'm the one who introduced them to each other!

Link never noticed you up to today, though. You've always been a shadow creeping behind him in the dark.

It's not my fault, okay?! It's not my fault that I'm insecure! You of all people know how often Ellie pokes fun at me for how I look! She's meant to be my older sister but it's like she can't stand me being in the same room as her! I'm always in everyone's shadow, never in the light! God's sake!

157

You're thinking of throwing your phone at the wall, aren't you? Yes! My chest feels so tight right now, this isn't love, it's bloody indigestion! *Then, leave him. You're better than pining for his attention.* Wow, y-you're actually being nice to me for once…okay, what do you want?

Nothing! Just for you to be happy and live the life you deserve. Wait, were you being mean to me to help me realise that I could do so much better than Link? *There you go! You've wasted enough years following after him, for pete sake, you need to find yourself a guy worth your time!* You know what? I guess you're not all that bad. *Oh really? Well, why don't you block his number and treat yourself to a shopping spree tomorrow?*

You know what? I like the way you think!

[NUMBER HAS BEEN BLOCKED]

And…done. Can you please get off my shoulder now? *Awww, but it's so much more comfy than your pocket!*

I sigh and pick up the whining mushroom by pinching its stem and delicately hold it in my hands. It blows a raspberry at me. I use my index finger to pet it softly.

158

It starts squirming from laughter. It's got the literal qualities of a dog or something. I give it a little ruffle on its cap, only for it to bark cutely.

Oh my God. It just barked! I must protect this precious creature. I know it was insulting me earlier but now, now it's precious to me.

The barking sentient mushroom must be protected at all costs.

"Awww, now who's being a gwood wittle mushwoom?"

"Q-Quit it, or I'll...I'll.."

"You'll what?"

"I-I'll make you think the world will explode!" This is followed by a tiny bark and growl.

Awww, wook how imitwating the whittle wooshroom's trying to bwe! Be still my hearwt.

"Hah! Nice try, little shroom, but you can't do that unless you're in my brain, and newsflash, you're not going back there to poison my thoughts again."

The mushroom's eyes grow wide. It's trying to get its way with its puppy dog eyes.

159

"Ooooch."

That was…the single most adorable sneeze I've ever heard in my fifteen years of existing. How is this little thing meant to be anxiety itself?

I watch as the shroom's hands come out of hiding from its flesh and form into a full limb to wipe the snot bubble away. The hand then coils back into the mushroom's stem.

I bite on my fist till I can feel my teeth compressing into my bones to stop myself from squealing from its uncontainable cuteness. It works, but now I've got a bite that looks like a vampire with the world's worst dentist bit my hand or something.

Oh my God- No, I must resist…the sheer a…absoloute cuteness…gah!

Long story short. I got so anxious the other day that I felt my ears pop and saw blood dripping down my ears, followed by this mushroom, that sounds exactly like me and *yeah I'm going insane, aren't I?*

It starts to jump cutely, which sends me into a fit of rage over how I'm forcing myself to keep it off my head so that it doesn't crawl back into my brain via my ear.

160

Stop whining, and barking and jumping and being such a whittle cutie shroom! I think you're literally my anxiety, why are you so cute?!

"You're still not going on my head," I quip, standing my ground. The shroom hops off my hand and onto my shoulder. It's the equivalent of crossing a canyon but the wittle shroomie makes it over in one pwiece *and what is happening to me?!*

It begins to nuzzle against my cheek. I smile at this, only to feel a slime running upwards my cheek. I run to the mirror to check if one of my zits has popped and...low and behold, the shroom is using its stem to climb my face. The gooey stream on my cheek is enough to make me realise it's using its cuteness against me.

I let out a growl under my breath and softly grab the anxiety shroom before it can climb into my ear canal. It meets my glare of fury at it as I put it down onto my vanity table.

"Stop trying to crawl back into my brain!"

It turns its back on me sharply.

"D-Don't you turn your back on me!"

161

I've never been more offended by a sentient

mushroom until now.

Last Coffee with Mother E

The rich aroma of coffee beans fills the air, I close my eyes, entranced by the sweet sensation of freshly baked pastries and cakes, as I watch the barista place them in the clear glass display. As I sit here, I savour the moment, take in the different scents, and appreciate the comfort of the café as the quiet atmosphere adds a sense of peace and tranquillity among the busy noise of outside streets. The *early bird catches the worm*, they always say, and I have caught the first freshly brewed coffee.

"Here you go, one caramel latte with cream"

I'm brought back to my senses as the smiling barista delivers the brewed coffee at my table and for a moment, I begin to feel happiness wash over me by tasting this delicious morning drink. The baristas are calm as the rush hour of people have yet to arrive as they create beautiful coffee art without any pressure. Sipping the piece of the art, closing my eyes to the warmth, I am transported into a peaceful escape for just a second as I look out the window and suddenly see small droplets tapping on the glass.

163

Hearing the rainfall on what was supposed to be a warm, sunny day has suddenly dropped a cold, shivering feeling as I feel tiny goosebumps rise on my skin. Unaware of the conversation I was about to have with someone so dear, I feel the sense of doom suffocate the air.

All at once, my thoughts run all over the place, anticipating the visit of the person I'm about to meet. *Her* presence fills the air already as the rainfall picks up outside and the sudden smell of flowers and trees get stronger and more powerful. *She* is almost here, as I feel the slight rumble and quake beneath the ground, begin to pulse stronger at every beat. This sudden strength in the atmosphere grows my fears and concerns. *She* is in pain; I can feel it. I start to hastily plan out what I am going to say, how am I to approach her so delicately without causing her more hurt.

Still, I am going to meet her and for a moment I feel blessed. How amazing is that? I've always wanted to speak to this almighty force of nature and to tell how grateful I am towards all that is done for humanity, protecting, and sheltering us. *Now's my chance to do exactly that!*

164

THIS BOOK JUST MIGHT BE BATS*** CRAZY

The heavy glass door opens as a gust of wind follows through. A small frail hand clutches onto the door for balance, as the figure tries to catch her breath a tiny wisp of polluted mist travels out of her. She slowly looks up, her face covered by a dark veil of steam as if she is hiding behind the clouds.

I look at her from far away; ocean blue hair that flows like endless river streams, forest-green skin that peeks from the corners of her autumnal coloured dress, she hobbles slowly over to my table. As she sits down on the chair, I notice the illusion of her beautiful features as the true colours become clearer. Her ocean-blue hair seems more faded than usual as little black boils appear on the surface.

I notice her forest-green skin, lifeless, burnt, and charred pieces of bark and ashes fall onto the floor. She slowly lifts her misty veil revealing her face which once an array of life and radiance is now sunken, lifeless, and broken of its shine. Tiny floating clouds sit softly on her cheeks letting out tiny squeaks as her honey golden eyes meet mine.

She stares at me. I look at her eyes closely and suddenly can see all the pain and suffering she has seen.

The earthy tufts that sit upon her river-like hair appear to be crunching and her ocean hair itself looks faded. I'm concerned for her health. She smiles at me, revealing her teeth, which are small snowflakes lined up in two rows, one below and one above her mouth river canal. She lets out a raspy cough as the staff brings her a cup of coffee.

I slip my hand between Mother E and the coffee cup.

"No thank you. I'll have water instead."

The waiter flinches in confusion only to then nod and retrieve the cup. Shortly after, Mother E is presented with a cup of fresh, clear water.

Only the best for Mother E, of course.

"I thought water would suit you better."

"Thank you, my child."

Mother replies with hummingbirds tweeting through her words in the calmest and most soothing voice possible. My face begins to slowly fall as I notice her clutching her chest in pain.

"Mother, what's the matter, what's wrong?!"

"I'm feeling a little faint my child, for I have cried my last song"

"Oh, I see. But what about the people of the world who are giving their help?"

To try and distract mother from her pain I decide to ask her about how her environment is prospering from the projects of humanity that are trying to save her.

"Not well my child, indeed it has been far too long... said and done and I for one am tired to go on. For humanity chooses not to listen to mothers' cries but instead push my limits, my patience, my gifts to their greed,corruption and lies. Till my tears of the rivers run dry, my skin crumbles and tears apart, my bountiful green beauty of forests burn, and my core existence beats lesser by day in my heart"

"But mother, surely those who are trying to save you, is it not enough?"

"Child, for it is not I who needs to be cured, not I who needs to be freed but humanity is the one that needs to be saved, from all its violence, corruption and greed. I have voiced my concerns, heard the animals plead, I grow tired of the plastic covering up my shores, the pieces of debris..."

167

I watch how reaches for a tissue to wipe the streams from her eyes. She struggles to grasp the paper into her shaking hands, trembles as she looks away from my gaze, trying to hide the distress that she holds.

That is when I take her bark covered hands in mine gently and recite to her my own song of nature from deep within my heart.

"Humanity will fall apart, if we do not see the damage that is happening, and wish to make a start, have a change of heart, to protect Mother E for our offsprings in the future to see, trees of green, oceans, rivers, streams, water all clean and pristine, animals thriving, pollution dying, Mother E floating in the sky, oxygen dancing in the air, life itself un-phasing away, ice caps living to float together attached for yet another day. We're the lucky ones to see all this beauty, but we've got to start preserving and protecting you, Mother Earth, for as your children, we have a duty."

Mother E cannot conceal the raindrops falling from her eyes as I finish up my performance.

"My child. I have never seen nor heard a more beautiful song than this."

Blood begins to rush up to my cheeks

"What about nature, trees, life itself?"

"It's people like yourself who wish for change that give me the strength to stick around."

No longer able to hold in the wave of emotions that envelop my heart, I rush into Mother 's arms. I feel her wooden hands embrace me tightly.

"I…h-have long f…feared the change of climate, my child…"

Mother E's voice breaks like the flakes of bark she leaves behind upon the table. That's when I hold her shoulders softly and look at her directly in her eyes.

With a reassuring look, I plead my case while holding her hand to let her know she's still got her children and a place to call home.

"There's more of us. We'll do what we can..I promise you…you *still* have a fighting chance."

Icebreaker

As I awaken, I find myself hanging from the edge of a steep cliff, covered by a blanket of snow. The snow was at white as cotton wool but the world around me felt as cold and silent as a burial ground. The thoughts of dying entered my mind, as if I were suddenly hit by a bolt of lightning. The chilliness of the forest seeps into my lungs as I take a deep breath.

I inch my neck upwards, attempting to look at my surroundings from the cliffside. I could only manage to notice the shadows of the naked trees, in the dead of the night, which looked like lonely ghosts, helpless, reflecting exactly how I felt in that moment.

The darkness of the night envelops me. I feel the palm of my hand begin to slip. I panic, trying to hoist myself up, but my foot suddenly gives way, the piece of rock that it was once balancing on, falls into the snowy abyss below. I needed more than ever to reach the top. I had to see her again. I feel my hand become numb from the cold air, the lashes on my eyes freeze up in the cold air's breeze.

"Tasha!"

I yell out, my voice becoming hoarse from the coolness around me.

There is only silence.

"Oh God!" I find myself screeching.

The palm of my hand lets go of the rock it was once grasping. I clench my teeth. *I have to do something or it all ends here!*

Without wasting any time, using all the strength I have left in my body, before I can fall, I quickly throw my right arm in front of myself and grab the nearest rock beside it, cutting the centre of my palm in the process.

I wince from the pain. My now exposed and bloody flesh stings as the cold air penetrates it.

My hand slips off the rock.

My body instantly thrashes into the ground. A sharp sensation takes over my body, flowing through my spine and downwards my legs. I feel each of my bones shatter. I lay there in agony, sobbing, allowing the snow to engulf me.

171

CW: contains depictions of body horror / death / strong language / descriptions of closed spaces / suffocation.

THE AGENDA OF THE DECEASED

"Close that fucking door, now!"

Cindy continues walking, ignoring Simon's screams. The only sound we can hear is our own heartbeats echoing in each of our heads. Si takes a step closer, tapping on the transparent door.

Nothing. *Okay, good. We're safe for now.*

Simon's next to rest his hand on the glass. For a few seconds, there is silence, but just as he turns around in reassurance of being safe, a decaying corpse appears in front of the glass, groaning. It smears its rotten flesh around the glass, leaving a dark cesspit of saliva trail behind its upper lip. One of its eyes is hanging from its socket.

We all scream in horror and take a step back simultaneously, only for Simon to remain standing near the glass door.

"Get away from it!"

He ignores my cries and rests his palm onto the glass in front of him. The corpse lets out a small grunt before extending its mouth open, revealing six sharp fangs protruding from its hard palate.

While Sophie cowers within Kyle's arms in pure disgust and fear of the corpse, which is now in the process of peeling off its own skin, Simon remains with his feet glued to the floor.

"Are you deaf, Simon?!"

"I can't."

"What do you mean you can't?! *Don't* play games, Simon! No one's laughing, alright?!"

He ignores Kyle and places another hand on the glass.

"I really can't. I-I can't leave her!"

Mate, that's a corpse...you...you good?

"Her? Are you mad or just stupid?! That thing isn't a 'her'!"

"She is!"

"No, it's no-"

"Don't insult Cindy or I'll fucking clobber ya!"

173

My fist clenches. I'm about to make this bastard into a corpse himself.

"C-Cind-...don't call that thing Cindy! I know what my sister looks like, alright?!"

"I know it's *her*. Look at 'er eyes."

"Look at her single fucking eye, you mean (!)"

We all shudder from a cold breeze which blankets our bodies.

"Anyone else feel that or...just me?" I ask while we all just stand there and watch as the corpse tears its hair strand by strand while a low snarl escapes its mouth.

After what feels like two minutes, someone finally brings us back to our senses.

"Oh shit! It *is* her!"

"No Soph, don't encourage him, I swear to God."

"John, I-I know that eye a-anywhere...that...single eye."

I watch in confusion as Sophie lifts up her finger and points in the direction of the glass door, which the creature sits in, trapped.

174

As I'm about to tell Kyle to sort out his girl, I turn around only to see Kyle pointing in the same direction with a thousand yard stare.

"Seriously? You too? Okay guys, quit it, yeah?!"

All Kyle and Sophie do is walk past me and place their hands onto that bloody glass door. I'm quick to point out the danger straight in front of them that they seem to be ignoring because they're idiots.

"Ummm, guys…?! The fucking corpse, maybe?!"

It's not long before Si, Soph and Ky turn around without their bodies moving. I'm talking about a three hundred and sixty degree rotation of their heads.

The curse…it's actually real.

Their eyes pierce into mine. They open their mouths and shrill violently. Their tongues stick outwards as they form a circle by pressing their hands inwards to each other.

CRACK.

Si's bone compresses into Sophie's hand. Both their hands hang lifelessly and limplessly. The skin that once sheltered their individual bones, pokes out of their now torn flesh. Then there's blood. In gallons. Submerging the…entire floor?!

175

They grin at me while the flesh in Si's hand swings like a tetherball. Sophie's hand falls off from Si's strength.. I look away, feeling my stomach about to flip over itself.

That's when I hear a crunch and look up to see Kyle d…dissolving his girlfriend's hand with his own saliva.

W-What the fu-

I blink. I'm in a white void. It's quiet. Nothing's here. I get up and walk around. No corridors, no walls, just…nothingness all around. I'm now running as the hairs on my arms stand up. I run as far as I can, calling out for them.

"Si!, Soph?, Ky?!"

No answer. Just *keep running.*

*

How long has it been? …How long has it been?! I need to know how long it's been!

No…one's…here.

I'm lying down hugging my knees. Haven't opened my eyes. Figured there's no point. Stopped running. No point. Stopped crying.

176

Gotta keep myself hydrated somehow. There's
nothing. There's no one. No one can hear me, see me. I think
I'm dead, but then how can I think?

I hear a loud BANG and flinch.

There's a sharp squelch sound followed by an owl
hoot. I open my eyes to see my friend's bodies lying limp.
The decaying corpse froths over the discarded corpses.
We're both standing in a pile of blood.

My breaths are heavy, my heart's thumping, my
mind's foggy. There's tears in my eyes, I feel like I'm
drowning from the inside of my own body.

I'm aching all over and too weak to move. The corpse
approaches me slowly, taunting me with its every move. Its
presence is like the poke of a needle to every inch of my
skin. The closer it walks over, the more weak I get.

I'm kneeling now, panting as my energy's been
drained out of me. It's as if the corpse has some kind of
vacuum cleaner in its mouth.

"J-o-h-h-h-h-n-n-n-n-n-n-n-n-n"

The corpse's demonic voice sings it's eerie song to
me.

177

I'm about to collapse from the pressure in my head. There might not be stones on top of me but there are somehow physical stones colliding within my head. I am not making this up. I can feel stones crashing together, slowly stretching the size of my head.

"H…ow do you know m…y…"

I try to finish my sentence, but my voice drops lower and lower. Through blurred eyes, I watch as the corpse's hand grows a branch which blossoms into a flower, but instead of being nice to look at, this flower's made of flesh with protruding veins throbbing inside each flesh coated petal. The flower then stretches the fibres of its muscles and tendons till they pop in order to convert itself into a long, slender, human hand that coils its freshly grown fingers around my cheeks. With the fresh hand covered in residue of what I think is placenta, the corpse speaks.

"M_ _ _ _ _ y…b-r-o-t-h-e-r-r-r-r-r-r-r-r-"

"C…Cin…d…y?"

My body turns limp as I'm thrown across the room. A shape follows me. I'm trying to pull myself up but my arms are too weak.

178

"W...what're y-you..."

"B-r-e-a-k m-y c-u-r-s-e-e-e-e-e-e-e!"

The corpse screeches loudly. I'm left seeing only red and black spots across a white wall. There's a loud crack. The ground vibrates beneath me. Below me becomes a damp and cushioned, silky surface. I feel the softness coil around my limbs.

A hand-like shadow emerges from underneath me. It begins to pull me under. As I attempt to claw my way out, the surface becomes tighter as the shadow's grasp becomes more secured.. The walls around me become coated in a honey-like substance like bugs discover in a Venus Flytrap. My eyes prickle with tears from the stinging aroma of the substance. Everything burns. I reach out for the surface, only for the surface to form into glass.

Kyle touched glass earlier.

The floors shift with a large THUMP. There's only footsteps. I feel Cindy speak through vibrations.

"A-l-i-f-e- f-o-r- a- l-i-f-e-"

What does she mean?! What's happeni-

179

The surface shifts in vibration pressure. It's too much for the cave. I become still with no thoughts and no pulse.

CW: Contains depictions of a graphic surgical procedure / needles.

Her Perpetual Turmoil

With every stab of the needle, she feels her soul leave her body. Surrounded by doctors wearing surgical masks and lab coats, she's conscious, yet as the metal pierces through her flesh once more, she wishes to be anything but. Calming echoes of a woman's voice whisper to her, yet she cannot hear them. She cannot hear anything. The noise around her is drowned out by the sound of her own frail cries. With more medical jargon spread around, the doctors ask her to brace herself.

Another hit. This time, seeping through the most sensitive part of the spinal nerve. Her pulse, now a drum, thumping, hollering as her body's response kicks in. Through her watery eyes, she bites her lip while burrowing her head onto the theatre table. She can taste blood. She can smell metal. The walls of the theatre are covered by her screams.

To add to the torture, she grows faint, pale. She is now weakened, physically, mentally, emotionally, not from her own tears, her screams, her pulsating heart, her aching headache, but from the raw pain of the needle.

181

It must be done. She understands this. The sedatives aren't working though, still, it must be done.

The needle slides itself into her spine once more. At this point she is no longer there. It is only her and God. She whispers to God in her head to make it stop. All the doctors can see is the girl scrunched into a ball on her side, wincing, defeated, tired. They see her teeth which grind into themselves from being clenched shut. They notice her physically shaking.

That's when they hear it.

"No...more...please..." she mouths, in pure exhaustion. The doctors pause and address the situation.

"We still need to examine further...can you hang in there a little bit more?"

A single tear sheds from the girl's reddened eyes. She whimpers, looking around, only to be guided back onto her side.

The doctors look at her, sympathy and empathy plastered across their faces. Within that, there is also determination. She understands what this means. She must endure the pain, no matter how much it burns.

She simply nods. It's all she can manage at this point. It's not the needle which has hurt her, but more the number of times her spine had to endure the pressure of the needle breaking her skin, intruding into the most sensitive and crucial area of her body, penetrating the core of the bone, removing tiny parts of marrow in its wake. The needle pleasures itself with her every cry, whimper, and scream.

Until it is over, she remains in hell.

Author's note: Shoutout to my two best friends who inspired this story. May this memory continue to live rent free in our minds for eternity. Never forget the beetle formation. This story's dedicated to the two people in my life who never fail to make me laugh even in the toughest of times. Love you both to the moon and back. Sad spider squad forever.

A Malfunction Like No Other

I remember it like it was yesterday (which it was). I approached the classroom with a gleam in my eyes and an all too familiar thirst for knowledge. After parking my chair in its designated 'driver zone' (being my desk), the lesson soon kicked off. The classroom was quiet, so quiet in fact, that I could only hear my own thoughts.

I typed away on the keyboard in front of me, and soon stopped to scratch my nose. I suddenly looked up. Beady eyes faced my direction, as I was met with looks of confusion and annoyance from my peers. Oh god, they're looking at me...why are they looking at me? A sudden thumping sound jolted my body upright. I soon realised why the lesson had come to a halt.

I reversed my chair outwards from my desk and glared at the beast in action. There my right leg was, spasming, kicking itself on the back of the chair, probably bruising itself in the process. *Please stop, this hurts so much!* It continued beating itself up, as my teacher coughed nervously while trying to distract the class from the funeral that was happening.

I remember nervously smiling back, glaring at my leg from the corner of my eye. What did my leg ever do to itself? *Stop trying to kermit during my lesson, please!* Alas, it continued its demise, taunting me in the process.

After blinking in surprise, another realisation hit me. My leg was not only banging loudly like a drum every time my teacher's mouth decided to move, but it was accompanied by half of the footplate itself which was snapped off from the strength of my spasm!

Somehow, my own leg somehow managed to snap a metal rod off another piece of metal...*what am I, Hercules?* I stared at the abomination below me, with widened eyes, half in amazement of my own strength and half in genuine fear of learning the fact my leg can snap metal in half.

185

Looking up, my class shared the same expression as me, while lost in the awe of what was meant to be my leg. The bell soon rang. I eyed my friends from the corner of the room. They walked up to me sharing a look of bewilderment. As I nodded at them, my leg flung itself into the air. The metal rod on the side nearly knocked out my friend in the process.

Our only mission was to get to the lunch hall without my leg committing assault on any unlucky student's face. How did the girls and I pass this quest, I hear you ask? By going into battle against the savage creature, of course! Without a moment to waste, I instructed Elly to wrangle one side of the beast while Lindsy took hold of the other side.

We headed out of the elevator and made our way towards the lunch hall. I stifled a laugh, while watching both of my poor friends do their best to keep my leg still and in control. Both Elly and Lindsy had to crouch downwards while walking in front of me, as if they were making the way for a queen.

To make matters more hilarious, they had to clear the way for me and my leg throughout Starbucks. All eyes were on us as we made our way through the open space of the college, exactly in that formation.

Realising the hilarity of the situation my friends and I found ourselves in, I couldn't contain my laughter and burst into a fit of giggles. I begged Lindsy to grab her phone out of her pocket and film this scenario, while tears emerged from my eyes as I cried from laughter.

I may have been laughing about how ridiculous we all looked, with half of my footplate hovering above in the air. Deep down inside, the more I think about it, I believe I was laughing to hide the embarrassment I felt while driving around the college campus with my leg suspended in the air.

Of course, naturally my friends knew this and joined in on the laughter as a way of telling me you're not alone, Alice.

Eventually we made it to our desired location, the lunch hall. The girls and I sat round an empty table that was spacious enough to fit my wheelchair underneath it. We started to eat our lunch.

187

When I told my friends that it was alright to release my leg from their grasp, they both faced me with a sceptical look. After I spent a few minutes persuading them, they agreed to let go of my right leg.

I really wish they didn't.

As soon as it was released, my leg had shot upright and slammed the table *hard*, which knocked over our drinks onto our sandwiches and all around the table.

Thank you very much, right leg, you really do pick your moments, don't you?

While I winced from the new bruise that formed on my leg, Lindsy leapt off her seat and screamed, frightened from the sudden loud noise. Eliy looked up at me with concern and quickly took hold of my leg once again, without me having to ask her to. We all took a minute to stare at the spilt liquid that ran along the surface of the table, before bursting into laughter almost simultaneously.

I mean, sure, don't get me wrong, our drinks were now spilt and our sandwiches were soggy, but I was just glad that my friends understood my spasm wasn't deliberate...it's hard to find people who understand that some days one of my legs become my worst enemy, other days, the other leg would act up.

I lived in a confusing world that depended on how my legs were feeling on what days. When I was sad, my legs would become tense but even when I'm relaxed, my legs would lack tenseness, but kick anything and everything that would unfortunately be placed in their way.

The most annoying thing was having no control over their unpredictable movements.

Point being, I couldn't ask for better best friends.

189

A New Type of Cringe

~~Old man's shopping list~~

~~-eggs~~

~~-bacon~~

~~-toothpaste~~

This is meant to be a shopping list but now it's whatever the hell this is 'cuz I got a hell of a lotta stuff on my mind, and mom's busy with her new boyfriend to call, Dad's watching the game, dunno where my brother's gone off to tonight, probably to some chick's house. Yeah, he *really* needs to stop going to random girl's places, especially the ones who have boyfriends, but whadda I know, I'm just a senior doing robotics, right? I've got nothing to offer except curing ailments of old people with specialised engineered mechanical limb replacements, right (?) I'm being sarcastic andddd what the hell am I even writing this for? Who's gonna read this? The counsellor said it helps to write? Where do I start? What do I say? Well, RIP to my old man's shopping list. It's now as jacked up as my head. Screw it. Let's get righttttttttttt into it, ~~duh duuh duhhhhhh JOHN CENA!~~ How the hell did I end up in Caltech?

190

Today me and Hailey hung out at her house. She worked on more of her coursework for Uni while I was chilling beside her on the sofa, catching up with the latest Marvel movie on Disney +. She was unusually silent today, normally I can't shut her up throughout the entire movie, as she would go on and on about how attractive Chris Hemsworth is, yada, yada, but there wasn't even a peep from her about the mighty Thor. Just this once, I didn't have to look for a mute button on her. I felt something was off about her.

The silence between us felt awkward, so I decided to break it by asking her what's wrong. She didn't say anything back to me and when I asked her again, she began to cry. At that moment, I reached out to her and wiped away her tears with my sleeve. God, I hated seeing her cry like that.

I remember way back in high school when a teacher asked us both to dissect a frog in chem, I was all for it but Hailey was having none of it and ended up crying the moment the teacher told her to cut open the frog. Embarrassed by the situation, Hailey ran out of the class while everyone laughed at her.

191

I remember running after her and finding her sitting in the hallway, in a corner by the lockers. I sat by her and wiped her tears with my sleeve, then pulled her into a hug. I stroked her hair as she sobbed into my chest. While crying, she explained to me she was vegetarian and by dissecting the frog, it would go against the principles she lived by. I told her I understood and later that day, we explained the situation to the science teacher, who apologized to Hails for putting her through that experience. Science class was never the same.

I could tell that whatever was bothering her now, was bigger than that day. As I held her in my arms, stroking her hair, I heard my phone ring. It was Abby. There I was comforting my best friend, while my girlfriend, who was already pissed off with me for missing our date the other night, was calling me. I wasn't sure how the hell I'd explain to Abby the reason that I missed our date, was 'cause I had to reprogram my robotic dog as it was having a circuit meltdown. She would hate that I put my 'dog' before her, plus the campus bus wasn't working and I just needed more time to figure out what to say.

Hails doesn't mind my robotic dog and thinks it's cool how I built it from the ground up, but Abby needs more

192

time to warm up to him as he scares her. You'd think after dating me for two years, she'd be used to him.

I reached into my pocket to hang up the call, but just as I was about to, Hailey held onto my hand and looked into my eyes. The same look she gave me when I found her by the lockers that day, the same look she gave me a few years ago when she found me in the middle of a breakdown the day my parents divorced.

She stared at me for a few minutes as tears continued streaming down her face. I stared back at her, trying to figure out what was going on with her. I didn't have to figure it out for long, as she straight up said 'Max, I'm in love with you.'

I didn't know what to say to her, so I just sat there like a total asswipe with my mouth wide open. Never thought, even for a second of our time as friends together, that Hailey had feelings for me. Am I that dense?! I mean, where the hell did that come from?

Anyone would think she's just joking, but when she looks at you, with *those* kinda eyes while grasping your hand tightly, that's when you know she's serious. Feeling that she was going to kiss me, not knowing what else to do, I pulled my hand away from hers.

193

She continued sobbing, but instead of comforting her, I got up from the sofa as fast as f and just stood there like some kinda cardboard cutout from campus spirit day. I stared to you know, just casually take in the fact that she's IN LOVE WITH ME, and just tried to make a move on me when she knows damn well that I'm in love with and dating Abby!

This was the same girl who I met back when I started high school, who walked up to me at lunch time with her hair tied up in a bun, who smiled at me with her braces showing and said "Want to be friends?" The girl who I used to hang out with on top of the school rooftops to play hooky.

The girl who I used to sneak out of detention with, who's seen me at the lowest points of my life…it's not like I've seen her as anything more than my best friend. The stress was getting to me, and Hailey could tell. She grabbed onto my arm and begged me to stay but I didn't listen. I didn't want to hear anything, so I just grabbed my jacket and left. I wanted to say something about how much I love Abby before leaving but my mouth was so dry after her 'confession' that I couldn't speak. I haven't called her since, and I don't plan on calling her back for a while. I need time.

I'm not sure how to feel about Hailey anymore. It feels like all those years of our friendship were fake. I feel shocked that she would stoop so low. It's like the Hailey I know now wasn't even the same Hailey I knew back in the start of High School. The moment she puckered up her lips, closed her eyes and leaned in towards me, my mind froze. I gulped as I knew what was coming next.

What's even worse is that ever since I left her place, ~~I can't help wondering what it would feel like if I did let her kiss me.~~

Why am I so hung up on ~~the kiss!?~~ Do I tell Abby!? Do I keep it a secret?! Here's hoping Abby never finds this, 'cuz if she does, I'm a dead man for even thinking about ~~Hailey's lips on mine~~ STOP THINKING ABOUT IT DAMN YOU.

~~I think I might've maybe kind of used to be in love with Hailey I guess? but I think I was afraid to admit it, not only in case it ruined things between us but also 'cuz I was scared of in case she'd reject me. Makes sense now why I kept on lying to myself for years that I was chill while she went out with other guys. I wanted to feel happy for her, but deep down, before I met Abby, I wanted to be Hailey's guy.~~

195

Abby makes me so damn happy now that I guess I forgot how I used to feel about Hailey. Never thought I'd write about my feelings at 3am. Damn.

Shut up Max, It's late. Yeah. I'm talking crap about the Hailey feelings thing. Abby's the one I love. That's not changing.

 I just gotta get outta my own head, get some hours of sleep in if I can and set my phone to wake me up early to prep for the robotics test tomorrow.

Peace.

Hey pops, if you're reading this, we're outta eggs, toothpaste, and I think I need some advice mano to mano before I go back for the next term.

Nine Lives No More

It is written in the prophecy that it is our duty to
remain with our masters even when their hearts are no
longer beating, when the darkness eventually takes over
them, ridding them of senses, abilities. As they lie as
shadows of their former selves within this reality, it is
promised paradise and eternal life for the ones who hold
the most jewels with them as they descend onwards.

In return for our services, us felines are promised the
chance to drink golden milk and sit upon the bedazzled
thrones next to our masters and loved ones. That is our
expectation of 'death', which each noble kitten carries with
them until the day we run out of strength.

We lay upon our master's laps each night, welcoming
death, looking forward to parading around crimson
silk-woven paths, looking up at the sky, which would have
one hundred variants of jewels sparkling above, some
small, some jagged, some rounded.

I would lay upon the silk paths, with my master
before me, surrounded by bowls of only the finest salmon
cut fillet, prepared for only the noblest of cats.

Oh, how it would be bliss, to remain with my master
eternally by his side, with my brothers and sisters standing
proudly beside me. Over in the horizon, across the golden
mountains and silver covered streams, my parents would be
there, no longer grey and weary but smiling and full of life,
trapped eternally in their youth.

However, when the day suddenly does approach, the
rivers of gold begin to disappear from my view as the
darkness looms over me. The sensation of the darkness is
sharp, like a thousand tiny knives piercing my flesh.

197

The view of my sisters and brothers slowly fades before my eyes as the salmon begins to rotten. The coloured world that was once presented to me, becomes bleak and overtaken by darkness.

My ears are first to slumber, followed by my limbs - No longer can I move any of my limbs as I lay in an unknown trance, defeated by death. My family, no longer there, nor my master. The life I was promised, now merely just an illusion of my parent's creation.

There is nothing within me anymore, nothing worth holding onto. The extensional dread slowly appears within my head, as I muster up whatever strength remaining within myself to physically think once more for the last time.

Is this what eternal sleep is? A life overwritten by darkness, an empty void of nothingness, all leading to my time ending?

I cannot reach my paws towards the rivers, or feel the sensation of warmth, can no longer visualise my master's face, as my senses suddenly leave my body. An overwhelming breeze of fear enters within my remains, as I whimper to myself, scared of what was going to happen next.

I am dying, now I cannot stop myself. I have to step into the void and embrace the loneliness.

Feeling regret, I draw my last breath. My body crumbles before me, finally at rest.

THE END.

More by this Author

For those that crave and await more horror and scares, my dear readers, the answer's right here! - The poetry collection that this writer used as her debut into the writing world!

'A Fever Of Frights' - Ebook for Kindle (Available now!)

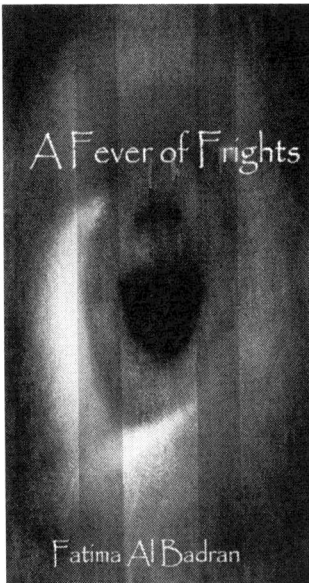

Things are not as always clear as they appear to be...

A mix of the strangest spine-chilling, mind-numbing, sanity crumbling, heart thumping, tales of rhymes to give a good scare or two!

From the web infested and cursed corners of a young poet's mind, comes unnerving ghoulies, haunted dolls to houses that feed on humans by the whole. These pages contain all, yet the question stands: Are you brave enough to turn the lights off after giving these terrifying poems a chance?

Printed in Great Britain
by Amazon